THE DOCTOR
OF
WHISKEY CITY

Book Four
in
The Whiskey City
Series

•

ROBIN GIBSON

AVALON BOOKS
THOMAS BOUREGY AND COMPANY, INC.
401 LAFAYETTE STREET
NEW YORK, NEW YORK 10003

.

PRINTED IN THE UNITED STATES OF AMERICA
ON ACID-FREE PAPER
BY HADDON CRAFTSMEN, SCRANTON, PENNSYLVANIA

For Jon, Christie, Cassie, Cayti, and Erin

Chapter One

In a small office, three men huddled around a large desk. The light from a single lamp threw a meager ray of light, illuminating the map spread across the desk. The tallest of the three men leaned into the light. His thin face looked even thinner and sharper in the yellow light. As he spoke, his teeth flashed white under the darkness of his black mustache. "Milton, you are sure they know nothing of this?"

Milton Andrews chuckled, rolling his cigar in his fat little fingers. "No, and if we act fast, they never will. Not until it's too late."

Hannibal nodded absently. "Fine," he said, then stabbed a finger at Milton. "Milton, you get back to Whiskey City. Start buying up the land, and make certain nobody finds out about this."

As Milton left, the tall man sat down, fingering his mustache. "Are you sure of this route, Rupert?"

The man known as Rupert shifted his feet and

1

coughed into his hand. "Nothing to worry about, Hannibal. The survey hasn't gained final approval, but this is the only practical route. Its approval is merely a formality now."

His eyes hard, Hannibal looked at Rupert. "You make sure this route is approved," he said, his eyes drifting to the door where Milton had just exited. "I think I will go to Whiskey City myself. I don't trust Andrews. I have a feeling if things get rough, he might turn squeamish on us."

"Hannibal, a thought occurs to me," Rupert said, then hesitated as the tall man's eyes bored into him. Rupert adjusted his silk tie and cleared his throat before he continued. "Once we have the deeds, we won't need Milton. He could be eliminated," Rupert suggested, a note of cunning in his voice.

"My thoughts exactly," the tall man agreed.

A feeling of relief washing over him, Rupert smiled and took a deep puff off his cigar. "I'll be in touch," he said, offering his hand across the desk. "Good luck, Hannibal."

Hannibal shook Rupert's hand, then ran a hand over his slicked-back dark hair. As Rupert turned to leave, Hannibal began folding the map. He folded it carefully, treating the paper with gentleness. He placed the map in the bottom drawer of the desk, and was just closing the drawer when the side door of the office swung open.

A short, stocky man stepped into the office, his entrance marked by the soft jangle of his spurs. He leaned casually against the wall and began rolling a cigarette.

Hannibal turned his chair, looking out the window at the darkened street. "You heard, George?" he asked.

"Yeah, I heard."

"I trust everything is ready?" Hannibal asked quietly.

The short man smiled, the long scar on his face visible as he lit his cigarette. "All you have to do is tell me who is first on the list."

"A man named Wiesmulluer. Run him off and make sure he stays gone."

The stocky George whistled softly. "Wiesmulluer," he whispered. His face grave, George rubbed his chin. "I've heard of him. He's a tough old bird. I don't reckon he'll scare easy."

Hannibal looked up, a hard expression on his handsome face. "Burn him out! If that doesn't do the job, then kill him!"

As George left Hannibal's office, Milt Andrews rode slowly on the trail between Central City and Whiskey City, Wyoming. He mopped his chubby face with a white handkerchief. The mopping did little good; the sweat continued to pour off him. It wasn't the sun, however, that caused the water to cascade off his face and down his neck, nor was his wetness caused by the fact that he wasn't a good rider and didn't feel comfortable on a horse.

Today his sweat was caused by excitement—an excitement that grew in leaps and bounds as the man calculated how much money he could make. The deal of a lifetime had been dropped in his lap, and he intended to make full use of the opportunity.

Andrews felt a brief pang of guilt as he realized he would be making money off of people who thought of him as their friend. His gains meant losses for them. The man shrugged the guilt away. Losses were a part of business. Besides, he was not doing anything illegal.

Excited and wishing to get back home so he could begin his conquest, Andrews urged his horse into a canter. A bleat of fear whooshing out of his mouth, the man gripped the reins tightly in his left hand. His right hand found the saddle horn and latched on with a death grip.

"Howdy."

He sawed back on the reins as he looked around for the speaker. What he found was a thin, neat man standing several yards off the trail. The small man had a book in his hand, which he shut as he approached the trail. "Name's Crawford," he said, tucking the book under his arm, then offering his hand up to the man on the horse.

"Andrews," Milt responded and took Crawford's hand in a soft grip. "I own the bank in town."

Crawford's face lit up as a smile spread across his lips. "Well say, this is my lucky day. You're just the feller I need to see."

Andrews tightened his grip on the saddle horn, his eyes narrowing ever so slightly. "Always happy to help. Were you looking to open an account?"

"No, no," Crawford said quickly. He put up his hands as if to ward off the banker's sales pitch. "I represent the railroad. We're looking to run a line through here to Seattle. I'm marking the route and making deals to acquire the rights to build across this land."

Andrews pursed his lips, running a finger along his jaw. "I could talk to a few of the landowners. Maybe set up a meeting with them for you."

"That'd be good. I'm going to mark the trail all the way to the state line. You can tell anyone who has these red flags across their land to come to the meeting. I should be back this way in four or five days."

"Well, I'll get the ball rolling," Andrews promised.

"That's right kind of you," Crawford said, shaking the banker's hand again.

"Think nothing of it. The railroad means progress and I'm all for progress. It's good for my business."

As he rode away, Andrews's brain whirled. He had four or five days; he'd have to work fast—if Crawford could be slowed down a little.

Andrews was still planning ways to slow the railroad man's progress when he saw the sheriff digging in his so-called gold mine. Poor Teddy, Andrews thought. A hard worker, but all brawn and no brains. No brains but lucky. Andrews's face hardened as he recalled how Teddy had dealt him out of a silver mine that was supposedly worth a fortune. A rich mine and Teddy Cooper had gotten it away from Milt for a few measly dollars. Milton Andrews prided himself on his business sense; he couldn't admit, even to himself, that Teddy had outsmarted him. Milt wrote it off to dumb luck.

Milton Andrews shook his head. The danged fool had a silver mine worth a fortune and here he was scrubbing along the creek for a few flakes of gold. To a man like Andrews, who detested physical labor, that didn't make sense. Of course, Teddy's mine was high up in the mountains and buried under a deep blanket of snow, but come spring when the snow melted, Teddy would be a rich man.

Milton started to call out to Teddy, but then his face hardened and he thought the better of it. He was still mad at Teddy, and besides, it was better that no one knew he had been to Central City.

Later that same day, George sat on his horse looking down at the house that belonged to Karl Wiesmulluer. George drew deep on his cigarette, studying the place. He didn't notice the way the place had been built with loving hands to last a lifetime. He didn't notice the porch built on the front which would be cool in the summertime.

George wasn't looking at such things. He was looking for signs of life. He crushed out his cigarette, flicking it away as he turned to face the men grouped loosely behind him. "All right, let's go," he said, his voice grim.

As they walked their horses up to the house, George untied several torches from the back of his saddle. "Burn the house, the barn, everything," he instructed, passing the torches to his men.

A large collie dog rose stiffly from the ground beside the porch. The dog's coat was shaggy and old-looking, and the dog moved stiffly as it walked out to meet the men. The dog sniffed the air, then barked a challenge.

George drew his pistol with some practiced ease. In one quick, almost careless shot, he fired at the dog. The bullet struck the dog in the hindquarters, knocking it down.

George smiled maliciously as the old dog writhed in the short grass, howling in pain. "Torch the place," he told his men.

As his men fanned out to complete their task, George smiled again. The smile still on his lips, he aimed carefully at the wounded dog. He started to fire but the dog jumped up and limped away. For a second, George stared at the break in the trees where the dog had disappeared. He thought about going after the animal, then shrugged and calmly built a smoke, watching with satisfaction as his men worked.

Chapter Two

In Whiskey City, even a spittin' contest has been known to draw crowds from miles around. Something real important like a good hanging or even a wedding, for instance, is liable to send the whole country into a real rip-snorter. Right now, we were braced for just such a wingding. You see, we were about to have a wedding!

I dropped my shovel, looking frantically at the sun. A feeling of dread hitting me, I calculated the time. Yikes, if I didn't shake a leg and get a move on it, I was going to miss the wedding. Eddy would peel my hide if I was late. Miss Edwina Wiesmulluer was my fiancée, and while she was the most beautiful girl in the world, she had a powder-keg temper.

Scattering my gold pan and tools every which way, I lunged across the creek toward my horse. Trying to run in the knee-deep water wasn't an easy thing to do, and somehow my body got ahead of my feet. My feet shot out from under me, and I pitched headfirst into the water.

On my hands and knees, I fought my way to the edge, clawing frantically at the loose dirt on the bank, I scooted up to my horse. Slinging water everywhere, I snatched up my gunbelt and jumped on my horse. Bent low over the saddle, I booted him into a gallop. We pounded for town, like the devil hisself was chasing us. Pushing a mess of wet hair out of my eyes, I clamped my hat on tighter. That's when I first spotted him.

At the time, being late like I was, I never paid that man any mind. I mean, he wasn't doing anything special. He just stood on the bank, and scribbled in this little book. Looking back on it, I wish I would have stopped and visited with him; it sure might have saved me some grief. But like I said, I didn't have time for such things. I just kept urging my horse to go faster, plumb forgetting about that stranger.

I barreled into town like a tornado, and even before my horse was stopped, I jumped down and started ripping the saddle loose. Tossing my gear in a pile, I turned and skedaddled for the hotel.

Now, I'm a big man and running don't come easy for me, but I was doing a fair imitation of the feat when I busted through the door of the hotel, nearly running Gladeys Briscoe over.

"Teddy, my stars, what are you doing? The wedding is about to start," she said, clapping her hand over her mouth. "Land sakes, Sheriff, you're all wet!"

"I know. I fell in the creek," I grumbled.

"Still looking for gold?" she asked brightly as I nodded, edging sideways. She smiled a wistful smile, patting my shoulder. "It's so nice these days to see a young man looking to better himself."

"Yes, ma'am," I agreed, trying to get to the stairs, but getting past this woman was harder than sneaking a lamb chop past a wolf den.

"I do hope you find your fortune. You are going to need some extra money. After all, you are going to have a family to support."

"Yes, ma'am. Excuse me, ma'am, I gotta go change," I said.

Her mouth fell open, but she quickly covered it with her hand. "Land sakes, yes! What was I thinking? You're going to catch your death, running around soaked to the skin. What you need is a mustard bath. You run up to your room, and I'll fetch the mustard."

"I haven't got time for that. I've got to get ready for the wedding," I said, getting desperate.

"The wedding?" Gladeys repeated, looking up at me with a blank look. She frowned, cocking her head to one side. Then all of a sudden her whole face lit up. "The wedding! Dear me, yes, you're going to be late."

A stern look on her face, she pointed to the stairs. "Young man, what do think you are doing lollygagging around here? You march up there and get yourself ready this instant!"

"Yes, ma'am," I agreed, taking the stairs two at a time.

I scooted into my room and slammed the door behind me. Then, on second thought, I turned back and locked it. A body never knew what that blamed Gladeys might do. I swear, talking to that woman was like having a sack of flour fall on your head. I guess I liked Gladeys, but she was dingier than a cracked bell.

I started peeling off my wet clothes, then stopped dead in my tracks, horrified by what I saw on the bed. Lying there big as life was a suit, and to top it off a necktie. Suppressing a shiver, I started undressing, doing my level best to ignore that suit, but it wasn't any use. It was like the thing had eyes or something.

Saying a cussword or two under my breath, I gingerly took that suit off the bed. Wrinkling up my nose, I looked the thing over. "Aw, crud," I sighed, knowing Eddy wanted me to wear it and that I was going to, but I wasn't gonna like it, not by a long shot.

Just putting it on was like rassling with a porcupine. I swear, the thing scratched and itched like some kind of varmint rash. Finally, tugging at that miserable tie, I stepped out on the street. Already, the town was packed to the rafters with folks, and more kept dribblin' in all the time.

"Theodore Cooper!"

My head snapped up so quick, it durned near came off its hinges. Standing hands on hips in front of the church was my betrothed, Miss Edwinia Wiesmulluer, and she was mad as a mashed cat. Even from where I stood, I could see the thunderstorm flashing in her black eyes.

"Teddy, get over here. They're about ready to start!"

"Sorry," I mumbled, scurrying over to her side. I didn't even bother to try and explain why I was late. I'd learned that it was nigh on impossible to win an argument with that girl. And while I'm big as any two men put together, I knew she was the one person in this world that I didn't want to tangle with. No, sir, I done tried that once and came up missing a yard of hide off my backside.

Right away, she went to fussin' with my collar, cinching that tie even tighter. I thought my head was going to pop clean off my shoulders 'fore she was satisfied.

"There," she said, stepping back, smiling softly as she looked me over. "You should wear a suit more often. You look nice.'' A fit of pure panic ripped through me. Seeing my panic, Eddy laughed, a sound that never failed to turn my knees to jelly. ''Don't worry, you don't have to wear a suit everyday,'' Eddy said, patting my chest with her hand as relief washed over me. ''But it wouldn't kill you to dress up every once in a while.''

''This tie is about to strangle the life out of me,'' I griped.

''You can take it off, if you want,'' she said. The words barely got past her lips before my hand was streaking to my collar. ''It's just that you look so handsome with it on. It would make me so happy if you would wear it.''

She stepped up close to me, and I could feel her shoulder brushing against mine. ''Aw, all right, I'll wear it,'' I said as she smiled.

We were walking up to the door when it hit me. She'd went and talked me into the notion of wearing that danged tie and somehow, I was happy about it. I scratched my head, scrunching up my eyebrows. Now, how in the world did she do that?

As we opened the door, every one of them old women in the place turned to stare back at us. Well, mostly they stared at me, with disapproving frowns. Turning up their noses, they went to whispering between themselves. I felt naked as a jaybird under their glaring eyes. Once we were seated, all the busybodies turned their attention back to the front, and I made a face at their backs.

''Be nice,'' Eddy hissed out of the corner of her mouth, then hauled off and nudged me in the ribs.

As I tried to catch my breath, folks got ready for the marrying, and the church quieted down. Now, I don't rightly know why I was so nervous, I wasn't the one getting hitched today. I guess just being in the church was enough to remind me that my time was a-coming.

All of a sudden, the side door flew open, and Gid Stevens, the groom, stumbled in. He stopped and blinked his eyes, looking like a man that's been drinking soured whiskey and eating chili peppers. For a second, it looked like he would bolt and run, but finally, he found his nerve and staggered up to the front.

Preacher Tom stepped inside, then turned around, spitting a huge wad of chewing tobacco out the door. Wiping his chin, he tried to slick down his wild head of hair, then stroked his beard. He stepped behind the preaching stand and looked the crowd over with a grave face. Satisfied that everyone was behaving theirselves, Preacher Tom glanced at his sister, giving her a small nod.

Poor Gladeys, she didn't have the foggiest idea what was going on. Right now, she was staring out the window, waving at a sparrow hopping on the windowsill. Preacher Tom sighed, looked up and shook his head. From the look on his face, I knew there was a string of blue words on the tip of his tongue, fighting real hard to get out. I reckon he didn't trust himself to speak, 'cause he walked over and tapped his sister on the shoulder.

"Oh, dear, are we ready for the song?" Gladeys asked, smiling brightly.

His expression tighter than a clock spring, Preacher Tom nodded, patting her on the top of the head.

Gladeys licked her lips a couple of times, then commenced to pounding that organ like a man mashing bugs. As Gladeys played, Mr. Burdett marched Iris Winkler through the door, stopping just inside. I had to look twice to make sure, but she was actually smiling. As a matter of fact, she even looked happy.

All of a sudden, Iris took off, dragging Burdett behind her. Now, for an old gal, Iris could gallop like a racehorse. Pedaling his feet, Burdett hurried to catch up. When they reached the altar, Burdett gave Iris a little shove, then beat it to his seat before they mistook him for the groom. Now, most days, Iris woulda likely scobbed his nob for that, but today she paid it no mind. Instead of tearing into Burdett, she just latched onto Gid's arm. Her back stiff as a fireplace poker, Iris waited for Preacher Tom to get on with the marrying.

Poor Gid, he was shuffling and shifting around, all tensed up like a man that was regretting the beans he'd had for breakfast. Right then, I would have bet my wad he wouldn't make it through the wedding.

Preacher Tom cleared his throat and looked ready to launch into his sermon, but Gladeys was still hammering on that organ.

"Gladeys!" he roared, with enough wind power to drown out a round of cannon fire.

Squealing, Gladeys jumped in her seat, snatching her hands away from that organ like the thing was red-hot. "Sorry," she said and giggled, but a fierce look from Preacher Tom wiped out that giggle in a heartbeat. Clearing his throat one last time, Preacher Tom glanced down at the Bible in front of him, then sucked in a full charge of atmosphere and took off. "Good folks of Whiskey City, we are gathered here today to unite these two fine people in the holy bonds of matrimony. But before we do, let's take a gander at marriage itself."

Preacher Tom leaned on that stand, smiling out at us. "You see, folks, marriage is like breaking a mean horse."

I gulped, scrunching down in my seat, remembering it wouldn't be long till I was the one standing up there. And I can tell you, I didn't like the sound of this.

Gid musta felt the same way, 'cause he gave a small yelp and his legs quaked like an aspen in a high wind.

"Like that bucking horse, marriage can have its rough times. Times when trouble and hardship are camped at your door," Preacher Tom explained, and even from the back, I could hear Gid swallow.

I was leaning forward, desperate to hear if that man could tame that mean horse, when the front door crashed open. The whole bunch of us turned to stare as a man staggered inside. His face glowed ghostly white and he clutched his belly, wheezing terribly. Stretching out his hand, the man struggled to speak, but no words came. Instead, he staggered forward, bounced off a pew and smacked the floorboards face-first.

Iris whipped around, her face looking like the wrath of God. "Somebody get that filthy drunk out of here," she snapped, just a hair away from really blowing her top.

Turley Simmons slid out of his seat, bending over the fallen man. "Aw, Iris hold your bloomers, he ain't hurting nothing."

"I don't care. I don't want some lousy drunk messing up my wedding!"

Turley turned the man over and slapped his face lightly. A funny look crossed Turley's face. He bent his ear to the man's chest. Slowly Turley raised his head, rubbing his chin. "He ain't drunk; he's dead!"

Chapter Three

"Dead?" Iris whispered, her tone as meek as I've ever heard. "I didn't know. Honest, I didn't know he was dead."

"Well, he's sure 'nough dead," Turley repeated.

"How can he be dead? I just thought he was drunk," Iris wailed, looking around the room for comfort, but no one was paying her any mind; they were all gawking at the dead man.

"Who is he?" Preacher Tom asked, pushing his way to the back of the church. "Does anyone know this man?"

Nobody else did, but I had seen this man before. He was the man out at the creek. "I saw him just this afternoon," I said slowly.

"Saw him? You mean you talked to him?" Andrews demanded, grabbing my arm.

"No, but I saw him. He was wandering around down by the creek when I was prospecting."

15

Andrews sagged into a bench. "Well, I guess we'll never know who he was," he allowed.

Louis Claude, the Frenchman who owned a farm outside of town, craned his neck, peering in at the dead man. "Who shot him?" Mr. Claude asked.

"He wasn't shot," I said slowly. Opening the dead man's coat, I looked the body over. "Shoot, there ain't a mark on him,"

"Then what killed him?" Eddy's father, old man Wiesmulluer, demanded. "A man doesn't just keel over dead. Something had to kill him."

"I don't know. Maybe he had a bad ticker," I suggested.

"Naw, snakebite," Joe Havens said, but we looked him over and couldn't find any bites.

I groaned as Turley Simmons stood up, a slow grin coming to his face. The self-appointed town clown, Turley seemed to think it was his job to keep folks stirred up, and he was right good at it.

"Maybe he's been an admirer of old Iris here," Turley said and placed a heavy arm around her shoulders. "Why, I bet he just pined away all these years for her. Then today, when he heard she was getting hitched, he just up and died of a broken heart," Turley said, chortling to himself. It was a good measuring stick of how upset Iris must have been that she didn't up and slaughter Turley right then and there.

"Oh, how romantic!" Gladeys said, clapping her hands in front of her face. "Just think of it, this poor man, yearning for years for the love he couldn't have." Sighing, Gladeys sank into a pew, her face all dreamy and her eyes misted over.

For a second, we all just stared at her. Then I shook my head. "We have to find out who he is. He'll have kin that'll need to know what became of him," I said.

"Does he have any papers on him? A letter or

something that might tell us who he is, or was?'' Mr. Burdett wondered.

''I'll look for those,'' Andrews declared, shoving folks off to one side as he dove down to the floor beside the dead man.

''He had a daybook!'' I said excitedly as Andrews pawed at his pockets. ''I saw him writing in it down by the creek.'' That banker did everything but catch him up by the heels and shake him but never found the book or anything else. The man's pockets were dry as a Sahara riverbed.

''Are you sure he had a book?'' Mister Wiesmulluer asked, rubbing his craggy chin. ''You saw it?''

''Yeah, I saw it all right. I guess he musta dropped it. I'll backtrack him and see if I can find it.''

''I suppose we should move him over to the livery and get him ready for a proper burial,'' Preacher Tom suggested.

''What about my wedding?'' Iris wailed, sounding like a lost little puppy.

''Oh, yes, of course, the wedding,'' Preacher Tom said, smoothing out his britches as he stood up. ''Iris, do you take this fine upstanding man to be your husband?'' he asked, gesturing at Gid.

Iris smiled, fingering her hair. ''Yes, I do,'' she said softly.

''Dandy,'' Preacher Tom boomed. Then, turning his attention to Gid: ''Now, Gid, do you take this lovely snip of a girl to be your wife?''

Lovely snip of a girl? Old Iris? I swear, that preacher man had himself a full-growed imagination. Either that or he needed spectacles in the worst way.

Maybe Gid wasn't sure what Preacher Tom meant, 'cause he sure took a long time spitting out his answer. It got so quiet you could hear breaths being sucked in and held as Gid stood there, looking like he'd just been whiffed by a cedar post. Finally, Gid swallered and commenced to nodding his head like a woodpecker.

"Jim dandy!" Preacher Tom roared, clapping Gid on the back. "All right, slap the ring on her finger, give her a smooch, and consider yourselves hitched."

"What a lovely ceremony," Gladeys said, rubbing her eyes with a hanky. Looking around, I saw half the women in there bawling. Why, even Eddy was sniffling. Now, what was that all about?

As the women mobbed Iris, Preacher Tom turned back to the dead man. "Now, let's see what we can do about getting this man moved."

"All right," I said, kneeling beside the dead man's shoulders. "Mr. Burdett, you wanna grab his feet?"

Burdett commenced to rubbing his back and backed up a step. "I dunno, Teddy, my rheumatiz has been acting up lately. Besides, I got a touch of arthritis in my shoulder this morning."

"Get outta the way, you lily," Wiesmulluer barked, his craggy face red as a mashed thumb. "I swear, Burdett, you got more things wrong with you than a dimestore watch."

"I can't help it. Got a weak constitution, that's all," Burdett whined.

"Weak brain, you mean," Turley said, cackling as we picked up the dead man.

We hauled him down to the livery and laid him out on a workbench. "We'll leave him here till morning. Then we can bury him," I decided, looking at the setting sun. "After that, I'll backtrack him and see if I can find his camp. Maybe he dropped that little book somewhere. That might tell us who he is."

"Well, shoot, we might as well mosey over to the saloon for a drink," Turley suggested, and since nobody could find fault with that line of thinking, we headed that way.

Somehow, I didn't feel right, just walking off and leaving that poor fella thataway, so I turned back. Poking through the stalls, I found a saddle blanket and covered him with it.

Turning to leave, I saw the banker of our town, Mr. Andrews, hovering in the door. Rubbing his pudgy little fingers together, he sidled up to me. "Teddy, I've been meaning to speak with you." He hesitated, looking both ways.

"What's on your mind?" I asked, watching enviously as the other fellers trooped off to the saloon.

"Teddy," Andrews said, putting his arm around my shoulders. "I want you to keep me apprised of the situation concerning this unfortunate gentleman."

"Huh?" I grunted, without the foggiest idea what he was blabbing about.

"What I mean to say is, let me know what you find out." Andrews stopped and rubbed his chubby hands together again. "I've got several deals going that should bring more people and more money into Whiskey City. Now, chances are, this man was snakebit or had a bad heart, or who knows, maybe he just ate some bad grub." His face dead serious, Andrews reached up and squeezed my shoulder. "However, if you should find out this man met with foul play, I'd take it kindly if you talked to me first. We can't let it get out that Whiskey City is the kind of place a body could get killed. It wouldn't be good for business."

I scratched my chin and thought it over for a second, then shrugged my shoulders. "Sure, I don't reckon there would be any harm in that."

"Good, good. I knew I could count on you," Andrews said, smiling. All of sudden the smile drained right off his face, and he turned the color of sour milk.

"Are you all right, Mr. Andrews?" I asked and grabbed his arm to steady him as he wobbled on shaky legs.

He grinned weakly up at me. "Just a stomach cramp. I haven't eaten all day."

I shook my head and had to wonder why anybody would willingly go all day without eating, but I could sure see how it would make a body sick. "Aw, fess up, Mr. Andrews, you're just getting to chintzy to buy food now?"

"Yeah, something like that," Andrews mumbled, absently patting my shoulder. "Excuse me, Teddy, there's a man I need to talk to."

"Sure, Mr. Andrews," I said, looking down the street at the man riding into town on a big bay horse. A tall man with a fancy mustache and even fancier suit. He didn't look like trouble, and I wanted to get over to the saloon, so I ignored him and took off.

Andrews nervously watched Teddy walk away, then turned to face the rider. "What are you doing here?" he hissed.

A contemptuous smile on his thin lips, the rider stared down at the pudgy banker in the rumpled suit. "I came out to check on things myself, and right away, I find that you aren't holding up your end of the bargain."

Andrews pulled out his handkerchief and mopped the sweat from his face. "What are you talking about, Hannibal?"

"I'm talking about that railroad surveyor. He was going to camp right outside of town. If he had talked to anyone and told them about this, we'd be out a fortune."

"Don't worry, Hannibal, he didn't have a chance. Something happened to him." Andrews had been explaining rapidly, but now his voice dropped off to a whisper, and the sick look came back to his face. "You killed him!"

"I did what I had to do," Hannibal said, then touched a spur to his horse, forcing Andrews to scramble out of the way. Andrews wrung his hands as he watched Hannibal ride into the stable. All of a sudden, the sickness showing on his face spread through his body, and Milton Andrews began to wonder just exactly what he'd gotten himself mixed up in.

Loosening my tie, I looked back as Mr. Andrews and the stranger had themselves quite a powwow. They seemed to be friendly, so I dismissed them and thought about the dead man. Who was he? What was he doing here? And most of all, what killed him? In all my days, I never heard of a man just falling over dead, and I felt sure this man hadn't done that. No, something had happened to him. I just didn't know what, but I was going to find out.

"You look like a man with a lot on his mind. What are you thinking of?"

I gave a small start, looking over at Eddy. I hadn't even heard her coming. "Not much," I said, shrugging off my thoughts. "What are you doing? I thought you went with the ladies."

Eddy smiled, giving me a small hug. "Maybe I'd rather spend time with you than them," she said with a smile. "But actually, the ladies are serving coffee and cake over at the church, and they wanted me to fetch the men to share it."

"Good luck," I told her, knowing that the men

were bellied up to the bar, and getting them to leave was going to be a tough chore.

Holding hands, we shoved open the saloon doors, stepping inside. Nobody even turned a hair as we walked in, being far more interested in that whiskey Joe Havens was pouring.

At the end of the bar, Turley sat cross-legged on top of the bar holding a bottle. "That danged Gid ought to be over here standing for these drinks," he complained.

"Aw, leave the poor man alone. Any man that's gonna have to spend the rest of his days with that old battle-ax Iris, deserves all the breaks they can get," Eddy's father, old man Wiesmulluer said.

It was no secret that he and Iris didn't exactly see eye to eye, but those two couldn't get along with anyone, so I guess it wasn't strange that they were always yapping at each other.

Wiesmulluer held his glass up to the light, looking at it thoughtfully. "You know, I'd just about as soon be that poor feller over there in the barn as Gid."

"Aw, lay off Iris. She ain't so bad," Louis Claude said. "I reckon she means well. You got no call to be running her down all the time."

For just a second, time seemed to stop in the saloon. Glasses paused halfway to lips and breaths were held as everyone waited on Wiesmulluer's reaction. You see, Mr. Claude and Wiesmulluer had been getting on each other's nerves for years. And over the years, they'd turned in some scraps that were legendary, but here lately, the two had buried the hatchet and were getting along.

When those two finally settled their differences, it cut the excitement level in Whiskey City by half. I reckon most of the town was just waiting on them to bust out of it and renew their squabbles.

Red color raced up Wiesmulluer's neck, and for just a second, I thought this was to be the time and place. Somehow, he kept from blowing his stack and even smiled as he clapped Claude on the back. "You know, Louey, I think you've been digging in the dirt too long. It's addled your brain."

Now it was Claude's turn to get red in the face and paw the ground. "I'll have you know that working the earth and tending crops is a far more righteous calling than playing nursemaid to a bunch of stringy, mangy, no-good cows!"

Well, sir, that was the trigger that tripped Wiesmulluer's temper. He slapped his glass down so hard that the whiskey jumped a good four feet into the air. "Mangy!" he sputtered, spitting halfway across the room. "You calling my cattle mangy?"

"And stringy," Turley reminded. "Don't forget stringy."

"No-good too," Joe Havens put in, licking his lips. "I know I heard him say your cows was no-good."

Grinding his teeth hard enough to crush corn into meal, Wiesmulluer pawed the ground, wiping his mouth with the back of his hand. "Mangy are they? Well, I noticed, when your family needed food in their bellies, you weren't above slaughtering one of my mangy steers and carving him into steaks."

"Oh, yeah! Well, the only reason we ate that flea-bitten critter is because you raided my corn patch. Why, you musta took a wagonload of roastin' ears."

"Roastin' ears," Wiesmulluer snorted, balling up his fists. "There was more worms on them cobs than corn!"

"Worms!" Turley howled, cutting his eyes up at the ceiling. "He gave you wormy roastin' ears?"

"I didn't give them; he stole then!" Claude shouted.

"I do believe he just called you a thief," Turley said, putting his arm around Wiesmulluer's shoulders. "You going to let him get away with that?"

"No, by thunder, I'm not!" Wiesmulluer roared, rolling up his sleeves.

"Dang right, you're not!" Turley agreed, slapping him heartily on the back. Straightening up, Turley slapped a twenty-dollar gold piece on the bar. "I got twenty on Frenchy."

Wiesmulluer stopped dead in his tracks, his eyes crossing as he looked confused. That confusion quickly melted into pure anger. "You're betting on Claude?" he asked in disbelief, taking a step at Turley.

"Teddy, do something," Eddy whispered, hanging onto my arm.

I'd been standing there just taking it all in, but now I felt beholden to do something. I mean, that old man was fixin' to be family. I dug down in my pocket, and believe me, I had to go deep, but I came out with a twenty-dollar piece and smacked it down beside Turley's. "I got twenty that says Wiesmulluer mops the floor with him!"

"Teddy!" Eddy's black eyes snapped fire as she stamped her foot. "I'm ashamed of you," she said, turning her eyes to her father. "I'm ashamed of both of you."

"Stay out of this," Wiesmulluer growled, then pointed at Turley. "I'll deal with you later!" he shouted as he and Claude circled each other like a pair of wolves.

"A fine lot of help you were! Betting twenty dollars," Eddy said disgustedly.

"You think I shoulda bet more? Twenty's all I got," I said, thinking she was mad because I didn't stick up for her pa better.

"No! I don't think you should have bet more. I think you should have put a stop to this nonsense."

"Stop it? Why in the world would I want to stop it?" I asked, plumb dumbfounded. Sometimes I wondered if I'd ever understand this woman.

Eddy cut her eyes to the ceiling, giving me an exasperated sigh. Crossing her arms, she tapped her foot and ground her teeth. Branding me with a last searing look, she turned to Preacher Tom, who licked his lips as he sized up the two fighters.

"Excuse me, Reverend, aren't you going to stop this?" Eddy asked.

"Huh?" Preacher Tom muttered, turning his head slowly to look at her. "Ugh, stop it," he sputtered, his eyes drifting back to the pair of fighters. He squirmed under her stare, scuffing the floor with his boot. "You are right, of course," he finally said.

Putting his hands on his hips, he took a small step toward the two. "Now, see here, it's high time you two stopped this foolishness. Shake hands and make friends."

By now, those two were jaw to jaw, and nothing short of a team of mules was gonna drag them apart. Shoot, they didn't even give a sign they'd heard Preacher Tom; 'course he hadn't spoke very loud, and I reckon that was on purpose. For when he took the notion, ol' Tom had the wind power to blow the hat right off your head.

Preacher Tom turned back to Eddy, his face mournful as a broken-hearted coondog. "I'm sorry, missy, but there's just no reasoning with them." He blew out a big sigh and made a *tisk*ing sound. "I reckon I've done all I can do," he said, bowing his head.

He held that pose for a long minute, patting her back, then whirled to the bar. "Give me ten on the farmer."

"You're covered!" Joe shouted from behind the bar.

Wiesmulluer drew back and cut loose a mighty punch that woulda downed a gorilla if it had landed, but it didn't. Mr. Claude danced away, taunting Wiesmulluer.

Roaring like a hurt bull, Wiesmulluer set his feet for the charge when the saloon doors swung open. The town ladies, led by Marie Wiesmulluer, marched in.

"Hey, they ain't s'posed to be in here!" Joe Havens shouted, pointing a shaky finger at the women. "Somebody tell 'em to get!"

"You tell 'em," Turley squawked, snatching his money off the bar.

Following Turley's example, every man in the place whipped their bets off the bar. Slapping innocent grins on our faces, we turned to face the ladies.

"What's going on here?" Marie Wiesmulluer asked, glaring suspiciously at her husband.

Old man Wiesmulluer took a quick step back, pulling in his horns. "Going on? Ah, why nothing's going on," he said, looking around the room for support. "We was just drinking a toast to the newlyweds," he added as every man in the place nodded quickly in agreement.

"Don't believe them," Eddy said, pushing away from the pack. "Papa and Mr. Claude were going to fight and the rest of them was going to bet on it."

"Karl!" Marie shouted, a warning flashing in her eyes. "We've had this discussion before. No more fighting!" Marie looked a mite flustered as she stopped, smoothing her hair. "This is a time of celebration. A time for rejoicing."

"Very well said," Preacher Tom said, looking severely at Wiesmulluer and Claude. "You two need to

learn that behaving like varmints is no way to act.''
He grabbed the lapels of his coat and looked up at the
ceiling. ''You see, learning to live like civilized men
is like breaking a mean horse.''

He set his feet and sucked in a charge of wind and
looked ready to give quite a sermon, but Wiesmulluer
wasn't in the mood. He turned his back and walked
to the end of the bar while the women toted in some
fancy cakes and set them up on a table.

Out of the corner of my eye, I saw Wiesmulluer
waving me over. ''Teddy, I swear, if you are going
to marry that girl, you're gonna have to learn her that
there's times to keep still,'' he said, giving me a serious look.

Now, that old man thought Eddy was out of hearing
range, but he was dead wrong. ''Papa, what a thing
to say. Mother has a right to know when you act like
an animal.''

''Hogwash. I'm a growed man. I can do as I
please.''

''Well, you certainly don't act like a grown man. I
declare, you behave like a child sometimes.''

''Bah, what do you know,'' Wiesmulluer said,
waving his hand at her. ''Teddy, tell her I didn't start
this.''

Now, if he thought I was going to step in, he was
plumb looney. Besides, I was more interested in them
cakes. ''Let's go snag some of that cake,'' I suggested.

''Hold it, buster,'' Blanche Caster said, wielding a
knife the size of a sword. Now, for a kindly looking
woman who used to help out teaching at the school,
Blanche was whipping that knife around like she
knew how to use it. She pointed that cutter at us men,
giving us a stern glance that I remembered from my

school days. "Nobody eats until Iris and Gid gets here," she allowed.

"Well, where are they at? I'm hungry," Joe said, eyeing them cakes like a wolf circling a new calf.

"Some slicked-up feller came into town. They was talking to him," Blanche said.

Almost on cue, Iris trotted in with that big feller on her arm and Gid bobbing along behind. "There they are; let's eat," Joe shouted.

Iris stepped up to the cakes, dragging that duded-up feller with her. It was the same fancy hombre who'd been jawing with Andrews. "Before we eat, I'd like to introduce my nephew, Hannibal Eastham. Hannibal just told me he has become a doctor. The finest doctor in St. Louis, and he came all this way for my wedding."

I durned near knuckled my eyeballs outta my skull, I rubbed them so hard. That Iris was sure smiling up at that doctor fella. Why, she was beaming like a full moon on a clear night.

"You're embarrassing me, Aunt Iris," he said, but he didn't looked embarrassed. Fact is, he looked more like a kid caught elbow deep in the cookie jar. He gave ol' Iris a little hug, then looked across the bar, speaking up like a soapbox politician. "Aunt Iris, I'm dreadfully sorry that I didn't arrive in time to escort you up the aisle and give you away."

"You'd have to give her away; nobody'd buy her," Turley cackled.

"Shut up, Turley," Marie Wiesmulluer said, scalding Turley with a threatening look, then promptly shoved the old trapper off the bar. "Go ahead, Hannibal," Marie said sweetly.

For a minute, Eastham didn't say anything. From the look on his face, I'd say his first visit to Whiskey

City was proving to be an eye-opening experience. Shaking his head, he cleared his throat, then smiled.

"As I said, I'm ashamed to miss the wedding, but I must confess that the wedding isn't the only reason I came here."

"Why, whatever do you mean, Hannibal?" Iris asked, somehow managing to look like a wounded fawn.

The smile slowly disappeared from Eastham's face. He hung his head and lowered his voice. "Has any of you ever heard of Scarlet Colic?"

"Wasn't she a dancing girl in the Longhorn Saloon over at Denver?" Turley asked.

"Not hardly. Scarlet Colic is a disease, which, right now, is sweeping across the West like the black plague."

"What's that got to do with us?" Wiesmulluer demanded.

"I'm afraid that Whiskey City is infected."

A fit of coughing hit Mr. Burdett as he grabbed onto the bar for support. "Is this disease catching?" he whispered hoarsely.

"Very," Eastham said curtly.

Wiesmulluer snorted, waving Eastham away. "And just how do you know that we are infected?" he demanded.

"Yeah," Turley said, slapping his thigh. "You may be the finest doctor in St Louis, but how can you tell by just looking? Don't you have to slap a feller down on a table and do some pokin' and proddin' first?"

Eastham smiled as I shifted my feet. Somehow, I had a sneaky feeling Eastham had been waiting for this question and even welcomed it. "I just completed an examination of the dead man over in your livery.

He died of the disease, and his presence here is enough to infect the whole town.''

"How'd you even know he was there?" Mr. Claude asked.

"Mr. Andrews told me about it, and since he knew I was a doctor he asked me to examine the man," Eastham replied smoothly.

"You're saying this disease killed that man?" I asked, frowning as I scratched my head. "That don't make sense. I saw him this morning and he looked fine to me."

For a second, Eastham's face turned white as a wagon cover and his mouth fell open. "You spoke to the man?" he asked, a slight falter in his tone.

"No," I admitted. "But I saw him, and he didn't look the least bit sick to me."

Eastham shrugged, looking relaxed and sure of himself again. "Well, sometimes the disease works quickly. Mark my words, this disease is deadly!" he said, his voice trailing off into a spooky silence.

"Deadly!" Burdett whispered, his face pasty as milk toast. "Somebody, help me, I'm gonna die!"

"Quit your sniffling!" Iris snapped, shooting a mean look at the burly blacksmith. "You ain't dying."

"Oh, yeah, what do you know?" Burdett whined, wiping his nose on his sleeve. "I been feeling poorly all week."

"You're gonna be feeling more than poorly if you don't shut your yap," Iris growled. "My nephew is here. Nobody's going to die. Ain't that right?"

Eastham couldn't meet Iris's eyes. He looked 'bout as comfortable as a man setting in Doc Plumber's dentist chair over at Central City. "I can't guarantee that," he replied. His voice was barely audible. "As I said, the disease is quite deadly."

His eyes wide as pie plates, Burdett collapsed to his knees, dragging bottles off the bar as he clutched his throat. "I can't breathe," he said, his voice sounding like a rasp being drug across hard wood.

Chapter Four

Eastham looked down at the fallen blacksmith, a flicker of irritation ghosting across his dark face. "Get up, Mr. Burdett. Shortness of breath isn't one of the symptoms."

Crestfallen, Burdett lurched to his feet, slouching against the bar. Muttering under his breath, he glared at the doctor, who paid him no attention.

"If we have this disease, what can we do about it?" Mr. Claude asked, looking concerned.

"Very little, I'm afraid. There are treatments of course. Sometimes they are effective and sometimes . . ." Eastham's words trailed off as he spread his hands in front of him.

"What you're saying is that the whole bunch of you doctors don't know any more than a pack of flop-eared pups," Wiesmulluer said, growling disgustedly.

"No," Eastham snapped, his calm breaking for the first time. With a look of pure rage, he glared at old man Wiesmulluer's craggy face. Finally, the doctor smiled, but I noticed his knuckles were still white as he gripped the lapels on his coat. "What I'm trying to say is, medicine isn't an exact science."

Eastham relaxed, pacing back and forth as he talked. "The disease reacts differently as it infects different people, and as a result, patients respond differently to the prescribed treatments. Some patients respond favorably. I've even heard of patients who fought off the disease with no treatment whatsoever. Then there are those cases when no treatment seems to help. The mortality rate is almost 50 percent."

"Huh," I blurted out, scratching my head as I tried to figure out what in tarnation he was talking about.

"He means that half of those who catch the disease will die," Eddy said impatiently.

"Quite right, Miss Wiesmulluer," Eastham said, giving Eddy a greasy smile. He cooed at her like a man trying to coax hogs into a pen. "Beautiful and intelligent, an enticing combination."

For a second, I thought Eddy was going to fall down, her knees going all slack as she smiled up at Eastham like he was a frosted cake. I reckon it was right then that I started building a powerful dislike for the slick-talking doctor. I mean, I was so busy wishing harm on him that it never even hit me that a bunch of folks in this very room was going to die.

It never soaked through my thick noggin, but the news hit the rest of the folks like a bull post. They went to screeching and caterwauling to the point that they liked to have raised the roof off the joint. Why, ol' Burdett went plumb nuts. Begging for a cure, he mobbed the doctor, sniffling and practically frothing at the mouth.

It was Preacher Tom's voice that calmly cut

through the din. "What is it that we can do to lick this thing?"

"Right now, not much. We will have to wait and see how the disease progresses," Eastham said, then looked directly at me. "For now, I suggest that we quarantine the town."

"What do you mean, quarantine the town?" I asked, shifting under his gaze and feeling the eyes of the town on me.

"I mean nobody comes into the town, and nobody leaves," Eastham replied.

If that disease had seen the commotion the news of the quarantine started, it would have likely turned tail and run. I know Eastham took a couple of steps back when Wiesmulluer pushed his hawk nose in the doctor's face.

"I don't know who you think you are, sonny, but when I get ready to leave this town in the morning, I'm going. If you try to stop me, you'll be the one needing a doctor."

"Papa!" Eddy shouted, glaring at her father. "That's no way to talk to Hannibal. He's only trying to help."

"Karl, sit down and listen to what the doctor has to say," Marie said, tugging at her husband's shirt.

Wiesmulluer done some muttering under his breath, but he let his wife pull him back. Just as soon as Wiesmulluer wasn't breathing down his neck, the starch came back to Eastham's drawers and he got bold as brass.

"I hate to pull rank, but I have the legal right to impose this quarantine," Eastham said, looking all high and mighty. He looked at me, a smug smile riding on his face. "And as sheriff, it's your job to enforce it."

''What do you mean enforce it?'' I asked, wary of the answer.

''It's very simple,'' he said, like he was talking to a little kid. ''If anyone tries to leave or enter Whiskey City, it's your job to stop them, using any means necessary.''

''Him?'' Turley snorted around the neck of a whiskey bottle. ''He couldn't even keep me locked up in jail. How do you expect him to keep all these folks cooped up in town?''

''I don't think that will be a problem,'' Eastham said smoothly.

''There won't be no problems, not unless somebody tries to stop me from leaving town in the morning,'' Wiesmulluer growled and received a cuff in the back of the head from his wife.

''Wiesmulluer is right. I have crops that need tending,'' Claude agreed.

''Dang right,'' Wiesmulluer shouted, shedding off his wife's clutching fingers as he jumped back to his feet. ''I got cattle that need looking after. Calving season is coming on, and I got things to do.''

''Calving season isn't until spring. That's a ways away,'' Marie reminded him.

''That ain't far off,'' Wiesmulluer said, a black scowl riding on his face. ''There's a pile of things to do between now and then.''

''We all have chores,'' Claude said, his head bobbing up and down like a pump handle. ''None of us can afford to miss a week's work.''

''You missed more than a week looking for my gold mine,'' Turley reminded him, laughing gleefully at the memory.

You never saw a place get so quiet so fast in your life. Heads were hung as everyone recalled their behavior. They'd raised a right fine ruckus looking for that mine. We were still rebuilding the town. I reckon no one wanted to be reminded of that, 'cause for a long time the only sound in the room was Turley's snickering.

It was Wiesmulluer who recovered first. "That makes no never mind. I got work to do, and by joe I'm gonna do it."

"Is it worth the lives of the people you might come in contact with? This disease is highly contagious. Just being in the same room is enough to transmit it," Eastham shot right back.

"Come in contact with?" Wiesmulluer hooted. "There ain't five people a year ever come out to my place."

"Be that as it may, we can't afford to take any chances," Eastham countered. "All the cattle in the world aren't worth the life of some poor soul you might happen upon."

"Bah," Wiesmulluer said, waving his hand and turning his back on the doctor.

"Karl," Andrews pleaded, "perhaps Doctor Eastham has a point. Maybe you should consider what you are doing."

Wiesmulluer turned to face the pudgy banker, a ghost of a smile on his craggy face. "If I lose this calf crop, I might not be able to pay my note."

Andrews's eyes flew wide open and his mouth worked several times. Snapping his mouth shut, he whirled to face Eastham. "Now see here, Doctor, there's no need to act in haste. Perhaps a quarantine is a bit extreme."

Murder blazing in his eyes, Eastham glared at the chubby banker, who quickly cowered away. "I've quarantined the town and that's final," Eastham said, challenging me with his stare. "And I expect it to be enforced."

Finally Gladeys Briscoe broke the tension. "My stars, we don't have to decide this tonight. The cakes are getting cold. We'd best eat them before they get stale."

"That's a jim-dandy idea, Gladeys," Turley agreed, sorting through the bottles on the floor until he found a full one. "Here, sister, have yourself a snort of the tonsil lubricant."

Gladeys's face turned bright red as she giggled, fanning her face with her hand. "Dear me, no, I couldn't," she said, glancing quickly across the room at her brother.

"Suit yourself," Turley said, with a shrug. He took a drink, smacking his lips. "Why don't you go sit down, and I'll snare us a couple of hunks of that cake," Turley offered, shoving that bottle down in his hip pocket.

Seeing folks heading over to the table where the cakes were, I hustled up, getting in line before they were gone. Quick as I tried to move, Turley was quicker and got in line ahead of me.

"That Gladeys Briscoe is a fine-looking woman," Turley said, his eyes crossed.

"Yeah, I'd say she was a right fine woman," I replied, a lot more interested in them cakes.

Turley was gaping back at Gladeys and not paying any attention, so I slipped around him and corralled myself a piece of that cake. Carrying my plate full of cake, I crossed the room to the table where Eddy was sitting. "You should get some of this cake 'fore it's all gone," I said, cramming half a piece of cake in my mouth.

"Oh, Teddy, be quiet," Eddy said, folding her arms across her chest.

"What did I do?" I mumbled around the cake.

"You know."

Well, she said I knew, but to tell the truth, I didn't have the faintest idea. The one thing I knew was that she would get over what was bothering her if I kept my mouth shut. Sure as I tried to say something, I'd go and make it worse, so I concentrated on shoving that cake down my neck.

I was just about clogged up on cake when that cheesy doctor came over carrying two plates of cake. "Here, Miss Wiesmulluer, I thought you might enjoy a slice of cake."

"Why thank you, Hannibal. You're such a gentleman," Eddy said, giving him a smile, then shooting me a dirty look.

"It's a pleasure to serve someone of your beauty," Eastham replied, showing all his teeth.

"You can't say that to her!" I shouted. Well, I tried to shout, but it came out a little garbled around all that cake.

Now, I may not be the sharpest gent around, but I worked enough cattle to know when somebody is trying to cut a critter out of the herd. I didn't have to be hit over the head to know Eastham was trying to steal my girl.

I shot to my feet ready to waylay that doctor right across the top of his pointy head. "Stand up, fancypants," I roared, balling up my fists. "I'm gonna whup you good!"

Eastham didn't get up, but boy, Eddy sure did. "Theodore Cooper, sit down this instance!" Eddy snapped, giving me a look that woulda put a frown on a hyena's face.

"I ain't gonna do it," I replied stubbornly.

"Teddy, you're embarrassing me. Now sit down."

"I don't like the way he was talking to you."

"He was just being polite, something you obviously know nothing about. Now apologize to Hannibal and sit down.''

"Apologize to that tinhorn? Not in a dog's age!" I roared.

Eastham rose to his feet, but he stayed behind Eddy where I couldn't get a good lick at him. "It's all right, Miss Wiesmulluer, I understand our good sheriff's anger. If I were ever so lucky to be engaged to such a beautiful young lady as yourself, I'd be protective myself," Eastham said, honey practically dripping off his tongue.

Eastham extended his hand around Eddy to me. "I apologize for upsetting you, Sheriff. It's just that when I see someone as beautiful as your fiancée, I must pay her tribute. I deeply regret that you misunderstood my intentions. Perhaps my choice of words was inappropriate. I hope that you will accept my sincerest apologies."

I stared at his hand, my head buzzing from all them big words and before I knew it, I was pumping his hand like I thought he had water in his boots.

You can bet after that, I kept an eye on that slimy doctor the rest of the evening. We finished up our little shindig, and nothing got settled. As the party broke up Eastham was still harpin' on that quarantine, and old man Wiesmulluer was still balking like a mule.

Well, the next morning came, and despite Eastham's dire predictions, the whole town didn't come down with the sickness. Fact is, except for a few sore heads from the party last night, the whole town was fit as a fiddle.

Now, I reckon ol' Eastham musta done some contemplating during the night 'cause, come morning, he'd dang sure pulled his horns in some. Fact is, he was sweet as syrup.

I figure Andrews had clued him in on the lay of the land in these parts. The banker probably explained that a man with good sense didn't cross Wiesmulluer. If that old man said he was gonna leave town, a smart feller got the heck outta the way.

Anyway, by the time I got down to the café the next morning, most of the town was already there. Eastham was all smiles, going around patting folks on the back and pouring coffee for them.

I soon found out that they'd up and talked him into the notion of putting the whoa on that quarantine until somebody actually got sick.

I snagged onto a cup and was ready to take a lick from that coffeepot when I saw Eddy come in the door. Eastham dropped the pot and scurried over to her. He helped her into a chair, and she laughed at something he said.

My blood boiled and I slammed my cup down. Mad as a squashed wasp, I stomped out of the place and down to the stable. I was still downright peeved by the time I plopped my saddle on my horse and buckled it tight. I wanted to go give Eastham a piece of my mind, but I figured I'd best backtrack the dead man. Still, I didn't care for the way he kept sidling up next to Eddy.

I led my horse out of the stable and was just swinging aboard when I noticed Mr. Claude out at the cemetery, digging a grave for the dead man. Glad that he had taken on that chore, I started working out the trail. As I backtracked the dead man, I found myself admiring his courage. He'd fallen several times, but somehow, he kept coming. Whoever this man had been, he'd been tough and he'd wanted to make it to town very bad.

I followed the tracks to the creek where I'd seen him the day before. I'd kept my eyes peeled, but saw no sign of the daybook. Dismounting, I studied the tracks around the creek.

The ground was sandy here and didn't hold the shape of the tracks, but I could tell that more than one man made them. Even though the tracks of the second man were mere blobs in the sand, I had the impression he was a big man.

Hearing the rumble of an approaching wagon, I turned, seeing Mr. and Mrs. Wiesmulluer. The old man got down, walking over to me, while Marie sat in the wagon, smiling and waving at me.

"Find anything?" Wiesmulluer asked, his hawk-eyes scanning the ground furiously.

"Maybe," I said, pointing to a spot on the ground. "He met a man here. Over there you can see where they talked."

"Yeah," Wiesmulluer agreed, rubbing his chin. "The second man came down the trail from the south, then left heading for town."

Agreeing with the old man, I tried to work out the trail of the second man, but the tracks on the trail were mixed together in a jumbled mess. Most of the folks who came into town used this trail.

"Whatever that dead man was doing, he wasn't prospecting," Wiesmulluer decided. "See, he never hardly went down to the water."

The old man was right. Whatever the dead man had been doing, he hadn't been looking for gold. He'd crossed the creek several times and walked back and forth on the bank, but never squatted at the water's edge, like a man looking for gold would have.

"I wonder what he was doing here," I muttered.

Wiesmulluer shrugged, heading back to his wagon. "He's dead. What does it matter now?"

"You're right. I guess it's just that something bothers me about this. I think I'll backtrack him and find his camp.''

"Suit yourself," Wiesmulluer said, climbing into his wagon. "I've got work to do," he added, snapping the reins across the back of his horses.

As they drove away I caught up my horse, leading him as I followed the trail. The trail was the strangest I ever followed. The man had stopped several times, walking in big circles. What was he up to? I scratched my head. He wasn't hunting. He'd walked right over a mess of deer tracks and hadn't even paused.

A few times, he'd dug small holes in the ground, and from the prints on the ground, I could tell he'd squatted beside the holes for a long time, sifting the dirt through his fingers. Beside each hole was a small red flag, stuck in the ground.

Jerking up one of the flags, I turned it in my hands, examining it carefully. What in the devil was this gizmo? Then I knew. I smiled, trying to smother a chuckle. Anybody who needed flags like this to mark his trail so he wouldn't get lost had to be the biggest greenhorn I ever did see.

I started to throw the flag away. Then on second thought, I stuck it in my saddlebag and headed out. A few minutes later, I found the man's camp.

The camp was empty; all that was left was the remains of a fire. Tying my horse, I crisscrossed the camp. The man had kept a neat camp, keeping his fire small and picking up when he left. He'd left very little behind to show who he had been or what he was doing here.

One thing I did learn: when the man came here he had a saddle horse and a pack animal as well. I could see the marks on the ground where he had set the packs.

I spent another hour prowling the area, but found

exactly zilch. Whoever the man had been and what he was doing here remained a puzzle. His packs and whatever he had in them vanished without a trace. All that remained to show the man had ever been here was a line of red flags across the prairie. That and a body in our livery.

Rubbing the back of my neck, I mounted my horse, pointing him back across country in the direction of my claim. I had a lot to think about and figured I could think better while I worked. As I rode up to my claim, I could see someone had been here.

The hair on the back of my neck stood up as an uneasy feeling crept up on me. Loosening the thong on my gun, I looked around. The only thing moving was a few blades of grass, bending before a slight breeze.

Getting down, I checked the ground round my mine. Well, it wasn't really a mine, just a hole I'd dug back into the creek bank.

Somebody sure had been here. They'd picked up my tools and stacked them neatly at the entrance to my mine. I could see where they'd even sifted through my waste pile.

Scratching my head, I scooted into my mine, having to stoop low to clear the ceiling. Picking up my shovel, I started to dig, when I saw something lying on the ground in the corner of the tunnel. Dropping to my knees, I picked it up, letting out a low whistle as I recognized it. The dead man's daybook!

My fingers trembled with excitement as I opened the book, bending in close to read in the poor light. I turned toward the entrance, my head snapping up as I heard the clap of an explosion. For a second the earth rumbled. Then the whole world caved in on me.

Chapter Five

There's something about being buried alive that tends to put a pucker in most folks' backside, and I was no different. To tell the truth, I was scared silly.

As the dirt cascaded down my neck I froze, my muscles paralyzed with fear. Now, right about then, all I was thinking about was saving my backside. I dropped the book and dove headlong for the daylight. My lunge left me short of the mine entrance. Before I could scramble on out the front, the earth showered over me, covering my legs.

Screaming like a schoolgirl, I clawed at the floor, frantically trying to crawl out of the mine. I scrambled only a few feet before a huge mound of dirt slammed onto my chest, driving the wind from my lungs. I was trapped!

The dirt rained down on me, slowly covering my shoulders. I don't know how long the dirt poured down on me, but it seemed like a lifetime. My throat felt like a skinned knee from all the screaming before it stopped.

By then, only my head and arms were free, and even then my mouth and ears were full of dirt. I lay there a long time, my whole body trembling.

Finally, my nerves calmed down enough that I could unclench my fists and start digging myself out. I wasn't out of the woods yet. If a hungry wolf were to wander by, I'd make a nice supper for him. Or the man that set the explosion.

That thought hit me out of nowhere. Remembering the explosion just before the cave-in, I knew this had been no accident. Somebody had tried to kill me.

Jerking my head from side to side, I shot glances all around me. I couldn't see anything, but that didn't mean that the man wasn't still around. If he was, he might be interested in finishing the job.

A wave of panic splashed over me as I began to dig. I dug and squirmed like a man possessed, stopping every little bit to look about. Behind every rock and bush, my imagination could see a threat. In my mind, I could see the man, just waiting until I was almost free, then putting a bullet in my head.

Finally, I dug out my upper body, but no matter how much I fought it, I still couldn't pull my legs free. Pushing against the ground with my hands, I arched my back, putting everything I had into pulling my legs out.

My arms giving out, I collapsed, pounding my fists into the ground. My body was ready to give in and accept whatever fate came to me when I saw my horse grazing by the creek.

Hope springing up in me, I called softly to him. He raised his head, looking questionably at me. Speaking softly, I called him over to me. He came slowly, and I held my breath. I just knew he was going to bolt and run any second, but finally he stepped close enough for me to grab the stirrup. Shouting at the top of my lungs, I slapped his legs, holding onto the stirrup with my free hand.

Startled, the horse lunged sideways, dragging me from the mine. I swear, that fool horse dragged me upstream a good twenty yards before he decided to stop. Not that I cared; I was free!

Jumping to my feet, I danced around, trying to shake the dirt from inside my clothes. I knew I should dig out the dead man's daybook. I even started to do it, but I couldn't bring myself to go back into the mine. Deciding that book could wait another day, I gathered the reins. My legs were still trembling as I swung aboard.

Fighting a case of the shivers, I rode back into town, the place looking normal. I could see Mr. Claude walking in from the graveyard, a shovel slung over his shoulder.

Mr. Burdett was working at his shop, building a coffin for the dead man. "Did you find the guy's camp?" he asked, looking up from his work.

"Yeah, I found it. Not that there was much to see. All his stuff was gone. His horses, his gear, everything was gone," I replied, toying with my reins. "Somebody tried to kill me," I added suddenly.

Burdett dropped his hammer, whirling to face me. "What do you mean? Somebody shot at you?"

"Not really," I replied, shifting my feet. "But they sure enough tried to do me in."

"Who tried to do you in?" Mr. Claude asked, swinging his shovel as he walked up.

"I don't rightly know," I admitted. Now, I never meant to say anything about the cave-in, but once I started the whole story poured out. Even the part about how scared I had been, and I had fully intended to take that part to my grave.

By the time I'd finished, both Claude and Burdett were grinning. "Teddy, how many times have we warned you that that mine of yours was a death trap?" Mr. Claude asked, shaking his head.

"A time or two" I admitted, hanging my head.

"We tried to tell you to take some timber and shore that thing up," Burdett reminded.

Well, they had at that, but at the time I never even dreamed that the shaft would cave in. Scuffing the ground, I frowned, remembering the explosion. "What about the noise? I heard an explosion just before the cave-in."

Mr. Claude shrugged, tossing his shovel in the barn. "The ground rumbles like that, just before it gives way," he assured.

To tell the truth, I felt a heap better. I hadn't liked the idea of someone out there wanting to see me dead. Yes, sir, I felt better, but in the back of my mind, I kept hearing that explosion. No matter how hard I tried to ignore it, I couldn't shake the feeling that the sound I heard was more than the dirt caving in. I felt sure somebody had tried to kill me.

Doing my best to push such thoughts from my mind, I led my horse to his stall. After putting my horse up, I stopped to pet the bay in the next stall.

"That's Eastham's," Burdett said, dropping his tools and crossing to where I stood. "Ain't it a beauty?"

"It sure is," I agreed, running my hand across the shoulder of the sleek, magnificent thoroughbred. I felt a hot wave of envy for a man that could own such an animal. My eyes fell to his saddle, and never in my born days have I seen such a saddle. Hand-tooled leather with silver everywhere. Without thinking, I reached down to touch it.

"Leave that alone!"

I jerked my hand back, whirling to see Eastham glaring at me. His face stiff with anger, he shouldered past me, snatching his saddlebags. "Didn't anyone ever teach you that it's impolite to handle another man's property?" he asked, giving me a snooty look.

"Aw, I was just looking at it," I said, sorely tempted to tweak his beak, and after the day I'd had, who could blame me.

Eastham grunted, jerking open the bag, rummaging through it. "Well, at least nothing's missing," he growled, snapping it shut.

Now, that got under my skin. I doubled my fist, wanting nothing more than to paste him right in the chops. After all, he the same as called me a thief. Burdett grabbed my arm. "Steady, Teddy," he whispered.

"See that you leave my belongings alone in the future," Eastham said, tucking the bag under his arm. Whipping around he marched up the street, nearly wiping out Mr. Claude, who had been standing behind him.

"Surly-acting cuss, ain't he?" I grumbled.

"He acted like he had something in that bag he didn't want you to see," Claude commented mildly.

"He sure did, and he ain't much of a doctor, neither," Burdett complained. "I went to him this morning and he threw me out!"

"He threw you out?" Mr. Claude asked innocently, then gave me a heavy nudge in the ribs.

"He sure did. Said there wasn't nothing wrong with me," Burdett said indignantly. "Why, I woke this morning feeling downright miserable. I just know I'm coming down with this disease, but he wouldn't give me the time of day.''

The big blacksmith stepped right up to me, pulling down the bottom of his eyelid. ''My eyes are turning yellow,'' he moaned. ''Don't they look yellow to you?''

''Oh, yeah, they look a mite watery, too,'' I said, doing my best to keep serious. ''What do you think?'' I asked, stepping back so Mr. Claude could see.

The little Frenchman looked a long moment, then shook his head, making a *tisk*ing sound. Mr. Burdett stumbled back a step, his face white as snow and his eyes wide. ''What?''

''Spots,'' Mr. Claude said, sober as a judge.

''Spots,'' Burdett whispered. ''Heaven have mercy.'' Nearly in tears, he looked at me, then at Claude. ''Spots?''

''Yeah, two big ones, right in the middle of your eyes,'' Mr. Claude said, almost letting a snicker leak out. ''Wait a minute. Teddy's got them too.'' He grabbed Burdett, jerking him close as they both leaned in to look at my face. ''See 'em. Two big black spots with blue rings around them.''

For just a split second the terrified look remained frozen on his face, then anger swept it away as Burdett swore under his breath. ''You're both going to be sorry when I die!'' he shouted, shoving us back.

For a second he stood spraddle-legged, glaring at us like a bull about to charge. All of a sudden, he snatched up a piece of rope and took a cut at us. Whooping loudly, we ducked away, scampering down the street.

''When I die, you're both going to be sorry. All of you, and that fancy-pants doctor too!'' Burdett yelled, shaking that piece of rope at us.

Still laughing, we stepped up on the boardwalk in

front of the hotel. Eddy stood in the door, shaking her head. "You two should be ashamed of yourselves, tormenting poor Mr. Burdett that way," she said, but she couldn't quite keep the smile off her face.

"Aw, we was just funning him. Besides, he brings it on himself," Mr. Claude said, with a snicker.

This time Eddy did smile. "I know. He's been in to see Hannibal three times already this morning. The doctor took his temperature and checked him out, but there just isn't anything wrong with him."

Eddy laughed, shaking her head, then turned serious. She touched Mr. Claude's shoulder lightly. "Mr. Claude, I'm afraid your wife has come down with the disease," Eddy said, taking the little Frenchman's hand as they sat down on the bench.

"How is she?" Mr. Claude asked, a hitch in his voice.

I kicked the boardwalk, looking down the street. I just never knew what to say at times like these. I might not have known, but Eddy did.

She patted Mr. Claude's hand, giving him a small smile. "She's had the medicine and seems to be resting. The doctor is doing all he can. We just have to keep faith. I'm sure she will pull through this."

Feeling useless as horns on a hen, I followed Eddy and Mr. Cluade into the hotel. Preacher Tom bustled around in the dining room, helping to fix plates for the sick folks. And there was a pile of them. While I'd been gone, folks had commenced to dropping like flies. Seeing me, Preacher Tom whistled and waved. "Sheriff Cooper, come here," he yelled, his booming voice shaking the rafters of the place.

With a last look at Eddy and Mr. Claude, I hustled into the dining room. "Have you seen Gladeys around this morning?"

"No," I said, realizing I hadn't seen her or Turley

since last night. Now, I wonder . . . those two? They wouldn't have? Naw, they wouldn't have.

"If you see her, tell her I'm looking for her," Preacher Tom growled, breaking my thoughts.

"Yes, sir," I promised, wanting to get out of there, but Preacher Tom had other ideas.

"Is the dead man ready to be buried?" Preacher Tom asked.

"Burdett was just finishing up the box."

"Good, get him loaded up on the wagon and get him under ground before we run out of folks to attend the service."

"Okay," I agreed. "How many are sick?" I asked, beginning to wonder if Eastham's idea of the quarantine might have been a good one.

"A passel. I done lost count," Preacher Tom said grimly. "It seems like every five minutes somebody new flops over."

That gave me a lot to think about as I helped Mr. Burdett load the dead man onto the wagon and drive it up to the church. Everybody in town who could still walk, which by now wasn't many, was gathered in front of the church.

With Preacher Tom in the lead and Mr. Burdett following in the wagon, we walked up to the grave-yard, singing hymns as we went. Preacher Tom stopped beside the grave, bowing his head as we placed the coffin beside the grave. His wild hair whipping in the wind, he cleared his throat.

"Folks, living and dying is like breaking a tough horse. Like breaking a mean horse, life can be filled with trials and rough times that can sorely test a man, but if a body sticks with it and lives his life true to the good book, he'll have a purty white stallion to ride up to heaven."

"Now every now and again, a body can get

throwed off that horse and find himself in the company of wickedness.''

Before Preacher Tom could finish his sermon, Wiesmulluer tore into the cemetery, nearly upsetting his wagon as he slid around the corner. His face beet red, he stood up in the seat, hauling back on the reins. His wife clutched the seat with one hand and her bonnet with the other, screaming at her husband as he tried to stop the wagon.

''Look out, he's gone plumb crazy!'' somebody yelled as we all scrambled to get out of the way. Believe me, right then and there it was every man for himself as folks stampeded, screaming and throwing elbows. Blanche Caster, who worked at the school, durn near ran right over the top of me. ''Outta my way, clubfoot!'' she shouted, giving me a shove.

Waving my arms like a man trying to prime a windmill, I fought for my balance, but it wasn't no use. The dirt crumbling under my boots, I toppled into the grave, landing smack-dab on my head.

I reckon Blanche got what was coming to her 'cause just a few seconds later she pitched over the edge, landing on top of me. All of a sudden, my world went pitch-black as I found myself caught up in a mess of her petticoats. I swear, that woman had on more bloomers than a gaggle of dancing girls.

''Teddy, where the devil are you, boy?'' I heard Wiesmulluer bellow. Truthfully, I sure woulda rather stayed hid. I could tell that old man had some kind of bee in his bonnet, but I reckon it was my duty to face him. Pushing Blanche off me, I stood up, spitting out a big ball of lint.

''What's the matter?'' I barked, trying to wipe the fuzz off my tongue.

''Somebody burned me out!'' Wiesmulluer screamed, his eyes wild. He wiped his mouth on his sleeve and stamped his foot. "They burned the house, the barn, the corrals, everything!"

"Who did?" I asked, trying to boost Blanche out of the grave, and getting my hands slapped in the process.

"If I knew that. I'd be kicking his sorry behind over the mountains right now," Wiesmulluer raved. "You're s'posed to be the sheriff. Now what are you going to do about it?"

I sighed, pushing myself up out of the grave. To tell the truth, I didn't have the faintest idea what I'd do. But I knew one thing, Wiesmulluer expected action. More than that, he expected results.

Preacher Tom climbed shakily to his feet, working his jaw tenderly. Once he saw everything was in working order, ol' Tom's face clouded up like a thunderstorm. "Wiesmulluer, you crazy old fool, you might have killed us all," he roared, gathering steam with every word. "We're trying to send a man to his final reward. Don't you know it isn't neighborly to interrupt a funeral?"

"Aw, what's it matter to him anyway? He's dead. It ain't like he's got anywhere to go," Wiesmulluer growled, waving off Preacher Tom.

They glared at each for a long time, and it said something for Preacher Tom that Wiesmulluer backed off first. "All right, get on with it, stick him in the ground, and let's get going."

Preacher Tom finished his service, but after the interruption, he didn't have the same enthusiasm, which sure disappointed me. By now, I was real anxious to see what happened to the man on that bucking horse.

I didn't get long to worry about it. Almost before Preacher Tom said "amen," Wiesmulluer was after me like a pack of wild dogs.

"I'll get my horse," I told him, already tired.

I trudged down to the stable, with the old man following along, muttering under his breath. The whole time I worked, slapping my saddle on my horse, he paced, smacking his fist into his palm. "Don't worry, sir, I'll find who did this," I promised. Not that I was all that sure of myself, but from the way the veins were bulging in his neck, I figured I'd best calm him down before something exploded.

Wiesmulluer turned to look at me, and for the first time, I noticed how haunted and haggard his face looked. "They killed old Mike," he said, his voice soft.

"No," I whispered around the lump in my throat. They'd had old Mike for years, ever since he was a pup. I remember we used to take turns riding the big dog when we were kids.

"Yeah, they shot him and he ran away in the woods to die," Wiesmulluer said, his head bowed. His hands were shaking and he balled them into fists. "We worked a lifetime on that place, Marie and I did, but it's not just the house and barn, it's everything else."

"What else?" I asked softly.

"All the girls' baby stuff, the watch my grandfather left me. Marie's furniture—her mother left her that." Wiesmulluer smiled a little smile as he shook his head. "Man, I had a devil of a time packing that furniture out here, but Marie wanted it, and I wanted her to have it. Now it's all gone!" The deep red color shot back to his face as he slugged the wall. "If I catch the man that did this, he's going to pay and pay dearly."

"Yes, sir," I replied soberly. Stooping down, I gathered my reins. Avoiding Wiesmulluer's eyes, I led my mount outside.

One hand on the saddle horn, I started to swing aboard when I saw Mrs. Burdett running down the street. My mouth falling open, I dropped my reins. When a woman built like Mrs. Burdett runs, it's an eye-opening experience, sorta like watching an avalanche, you can believe me on that.

"Sheriff! Sheriff!" she screamed, waving her hanky over her head.

Stepping around my horse, I grabbed her in my arms, pulling her to a stop. I reckon if I hadn't helped her, she woulda been a mile outside of town before she got whoaed.

"What's the rush?" I asked, still holding her up.

"It's the land office," she gasped, trying to get her breath. "Somebody robbed the land office and killed poor Leland."

Chapter Six

The inside of the land office was sure a mess. A tornado ripping through the place might have done more damage, but not much.

In the back corner of the office lay Leland Smith, his arms thrown wide and his mouth hanging open. His face was pinched up and his sightless eyes bulged from their sockets.

His expression tight, Eastham bent over the body. "Is he dead?" I asked, already sure of the answer.

"Yes," Eastham answered stiffly. "I'm afraid the disease has claimed yet another victim."

"The disease?" I questioned, looking at the mess of scattered paper on the floor. "What about all of this?" I asked, gesturing at the room with a sweep of my arm.

Eastham shrugged, pulling Leland's coat together and buttoning it tightly around the old man's thin chest. "In acute cases, as this surely must have been to have brought on death so quickly, convulsions are quite common.''

''Convulsions?'' I echoed.

''He means gagging and flopping around,'' Preacher Tom supplied grimly. ''You think Leland done all this by himself?''

Again Eastham shrugged. ''I don't see why not. A man going into convulsions in a small room such as this is bound to knock a few things over.''

''Knock a few things over?'' I asked. ''He knocked a bunch of stuff over.''

''That he did,'' Eastham agreed. ''All I know for sure is the disease is what killed him. As you can see, he doesn't have a mark on him.''

Frowning, I looked doubtfully around the tiny office. Shelves were torn from the walls, and a chair overturned in the corner. ''Could a dying man really do this much damage?'' I wondered.

''Look at the man's face, Sheriff!'' Eastham snapped. ''He was in agony when he died. Perhaps now you can appreciate why I so strongly recommended that we quarantine the town.''

I didn't have an answer to that one, my mind busy picturing poor old Leland as he died, clutching his throat and staggering around this tiny room. It wasn't a pretty picture, and I felt a shiver race up and down my spine.

''It must have hit him just as he came to work,'' I decided.

''What makes you say that?'' Eastham asked, looking up at me curiously.

''He still has his coat on,'' I replied, pointing to the body. ''First thing Leland does every morning is take off his coat and hang it up.''

''Interesting,'' Eastham muttered, bending down beside the body. ''We should get him over to the livery and get him buried as soon as possible. If someone would help me?''

''Could a person catch this disease by handling the body of somebody killed by it?'' Burdett asked, wringing his hands.

''Quiet possibly,'' Eastham answered, nodding his head. ''That's why I want to get this man buried as soon as possible, to lessen that very risk. Now, would someone please help me?''

Boy, you never saw so many folks get so busy so fast in all your days. Why, in two shakes, me and Eastham were alone in the office. Glaring at the folks funneling out the door, I bent beside Eastham. A squeamish feeling crawling over my skin, I took the dead man's legs.

Together, me and Eastham packed Leland to the stable. I must say, it pleased me to watch Eastham's face turn red, and the breath whistle in and out of his mouth. I don't reckon he was used to totin' many loads, even one as light as poor Leland. I felt sorry for Leland, the man had been the closest thing Whiskey City ever had to a true gentleman.

Burdett flocked behind us as we gently placed Leland on the table. ''I'll build the box for him, but I won't put him in it!'' Burdett declared, keeping his distance.

''Fine,'' Eastham snapped, straightening his coat. ''Just see that you get it done today.''

Shaking his fist, Burdett grumbled under his breath as the big doctor marched away. ''Why, that persnickety polecat, one of these days, I'm gonna paste that sore head of his.''

''He needs takin' down a peg or two,'' I agreed, frantically washing my hands in the horse trough. Just thinking about what Eastham said about catching the disease from a dead man gave me the jeebers. Snatching up the soap, I washed some more.

I was of a mind to do some more scrubbing, but I could see old man Wiesmulluer prowling the hotel porch. Flipping the water from my hands, I scooted over to him.

"You ready?" he said with a growl, and I nodded. "Wait right here, I'll go fetch Marie."

"Yes, sir," I said, stepping around to untie my horse from the hitching rail. Through the window of the café, I could see Eastham sitting at a table, drinking coffee. I swear, all the women of the town were fluttering around him like hens after a prize rooster.

Grumbling to myself, and wishing all sorts of harm on Eastham's shiny head, I poked a foot in the stirrup.

"Sheriff! Sheriff!"

Startled, my horse jumped sideways, dragging me to my knees. Muttering a few choice words, I snatched my hat from the ground and climbed to my feet.

"Sheriff, I gotta talk to you," Preacher Tom roared, sliding to a stop beside me.

"What is it, Padre?" I asked, shooting a dark look at my horse. One of these days, I was going to learn that fool critter to stand still.

"It's Gladeys!" Preacher Tom shouted, nearly blasting my eardrums right outta my head. "She's missing!"

"What do you mean, missing?" I asked, digging a finger in my ear.

"I mean she's gone, poof, presto, disappeared," Preacher Tom shouted, grabbing me by the arm. "Let's go. We got to find her!"

"Hold it!" Wiesmulluer thundered from the door of the hotel. "Teddy's going with me."

His expression as wild as his hair, Preacher Tom

whirled to face Wiesmulluer. "Your burned-out old shack can wait. My sister is missing." Preacher Tom shook his head. "Poor Gladeys. She ain't all there, you know. Lord knows, I try to look out for her, but it ain't easy."

"Don't you worry, Reverend, we'll find her," I said, and I had a good idea where to find her. I turned to Wiesmulluer. "You and Marie go ahead. I'll help find Gladeys, then catch up to you."

For a second, I thought Wiesmulluer would blow a seam, but all of a sudden he turned and stomped to his wagon. "You just see that you do!"

An uneasy feeling on me, I watched Wiesmulluer drive his wagon out of town. "Sheriff, let's go," Preacher Tom urged.

"Where all have you looked?" I asked.

"I don't rightly remember," Preacher Tom stammered. "I done some looking around, and she ain't here."

"Let's go through the town from top to bottom. You start at one end, and I'll start at the other."

Preacher Tom took off at a dead run, even before I finished talking. I had to smile; ol' Tom had gumption enough for ten men. Still grinning, I trudged up to Turley's old dugout. I had an idea that after the way Turley and Gladeys had been carrying on, I might find them there.

At the door, I paused, suddenly embarrassed. Running a finger around my collar, I looked down toward town. "Turley," I hissed, leaning in close to the door.

I couldn't hear a sound from inside, so I knocked, then pushed the door open. "Turley," I whispered, poking my head inside. I felt a great deal of relief when I saw the place was empty.

Pulling the door closed behind me, I backed slowly out of the cabin. I scratched my head. Now where in the world were those two? With them, there was no telling. Starting to get just a bit worried, I hustled back to town.

We went through the town from stem to stern, but we never found either Gladeys or Turley. By that time, Preacher Tom was about to have a conniption fit.

I reckon he was about ready to take the plunge off the deep end, when Turley and Gladeys, calm as you please, rode slowly into town. His mouth dropping open a foot, Preacher Tom stared at them.

"Gladeys, are you all right?" Preacher Tom shouted. "Where in the world have you been?"

"Turley has been showing me around," Gladeys replied cheerfully, her cheeks a mite flushed.

"What!" Preacher Tom shouted, advancing slowly toward the pair. "You mean to tell me that while I've been worried sick about you, that you've been out carousing with this trapper?"

"You bet!" Turley chirped up. "We had ourselves a grand time. Gladeys is a whale of a gal."

Now, I reckon Turley meant to be complementary, but Preacher Tom sure didn't take it thataway. Growling an oath and slobbering at the mouth, he grabbed Turley's leg and flipped the old trapper out of the saddle.

Cussing some himself, Turley lunged off the ground in a low dive, grabbing Preacher Tom around the waist and pulling him to the ground.

For a preacher man, Tom knew a thing or two about fighting. He tried to bite Turley's nose, then knee him. Avoiding the knee, Turley grabbed Tom's hair, head-butting the preacher in the face.

Howling like a banshee, Preacher Tom backed away, clawing at his face. Setting his feet, he spat in both hands, then doubled up his fists.

I tell you, this was shaping up to be a rip-snorter of a fight, but then Iris had to shove her skinny nose into things. "Stop this nonsense! Both of you," she ordered. "Brawling in the streets, Reverend, I'm ashamed of you."

Preacher Tom ignored her, making a charge at Turley. Burdett and Gladeys grabbed him, holding him back. Turley jumped to meet the charge, but I snared him around the neck. Planting my feet in the street, I held on for dear life, while Turley flayed away with his fists and spun his boots in the streets.

Finally, they both calmed down. They walked away from each other, still snapping and snarling like a couple of wild dogs. Turley and Tom weren't fighting anymore, but the fireworks weren't over.

Her face stiff as new boots, Iris planted herself right square in front of me. "See here, Sheriff. It's your job to keep the peace. We are trying to persuade my nephew to set up practice here. This kind of vulgar display does not help our cause. See that it doesn't happen again."

Sticking her nose in the air, Iris sashayed into the hotel. I swear, that old bat acted like she owned the whole blamed town.

Too tired to get real mad, I sat down on the boardwalk, taking off my hat and wiping the sweat from my brow.

"No rest for the wicked, huh?" Eddy asked, laughing as she sat down beside me. She put her arms around my shoulders, giving me a small hug. "You look ready to drop."

"I feel ready to drop," I agreed, looking at the sun, which was ready to set. "I still have to go out to your folks' place."

"I was going to go out and help clean up, but I

couldn't face it. Everything's gone. Who would do such a thing?''

I took her small hand in mine. "I don't know, but I aim to find out," I promised.

Eddy managed a small grin, wiping a tear from her eye. "You better get a move on it. Pa will be beside himself if you are late."

"You're right about that," I agreed, getting to my feet. "You going to be all right?" I asked, helping Eddy up.

"Sure, I'll be fine. I promised to help the doctor so I best go."

I watched her hurry into the saloon, then crossed to my horse. "Well, boy, let's get going," I muttered, swinging into the saddle.

As we rode by the livery, Burdett waved us down, flapping his arms like he wanted to fly. "I finished Leland's coffin. You want to put him in it?"

"Sure," I said, grunting tiredly. Dropping from the saddle, I crossed to Leland's body. I looked him up and down, trying to figure out how to grab him. I didn't really want to just bear-hug him. To tell the truth, I didn't really want to touch him.

"Go ahead, pile him in there so I can nail the lid on," Burdett urged.

"I'm going to. Just give me a minute," I barked, waving him away.

"Holy moly! What the devil is that all about?" Burdett exclaimed as I bent over Leland.

"What?" I asked, jerking around to see Wiesmulluer's wagon tearing down the street.

"He just left. What in the world is he doing back?" Burdett wondered.

"I don't know," I muttered, trotting up the street. The way things were going, it couldn't be good. A feeling of dread on me, I stepped up my pace. I was running flat out by the time I reached the wagon.

Chapter Seven

Mr. Wiesmulluer stood up in his wagon, holding his wife's limp body in his arms. A crowd gathered around the wagon, straining to see.

"Doctor, you gotta help her," he wailed.

"Of course, get her inside," Eastham said, holding open the hotel door. "What happened?"

"We was driving along, and she just keeled over holding her stomach," Wiesmulluer said, his face gray. "I shoulda listened," he mumbled, then grabbed Eastham by the front of the doctor's fancy coat. "Don't let her die," he begged.

"I'll do all I can," Eastham promised, his tone kindly.

"Don't worry, sir, I'm sure she will be fine," I said. I felt like putting my arm around him, but I had the feeling he'd slug me. Instead, I stood there, shifting my feet, cursing myself because I couldn't think of anything to say. I wished Eddy was here. She always knew just what to do or say, but she was inside, helping the doctor.

"I'll go put your horses up," I finally stammered.

"I'll do it," Wiesmulluer barked.

"You sure?" I asked. "You don't look so hot yourself." And it was true, he looked like death in a skillet.

"I can manage," he replied stiffly.

I don't reckon he wanted my help, but I tagged along anyway. By the time we tended the stock, it was clear that the disease had its hooks in him. He was already bent over like a horseshoe.

"Let me help you up to the hotel, so the doc can check you out," I offered, and got my hand slapped in the processes.

"Let me alone. I'll be all right. I just need something to eat, that's all."

Let me tell you, that old man was grittier than creek water, but he didn't make it to the hotel before that disease put him to his knees.

Despite his feeble protests, I slung him over my shoulder like a sack of 'tators and hauled him up to the hotel. We musta made quite a sight, cause Wiesmulluer didn't go easy. No, sir, he kicked and screamed the whole way. But by then he was so weak, that was about all he could do. We were barely inside the door of the hotel when we ran into Eastham.

"See here, Sheriff. That's no way to treat a sick man," Eastham said, helping me sit the old man down in a chair.

"I was only trying to help."

"I don't need your help, thank you."

Well, maybe Eastham didn't need my help right then, but by morning he sure did. By morning, over half the town had come down with the disease. Even

Iris was sick, and that was a shocker. I never dreamed any disease would have the gumption to tackle her.

Eastham was running around, trying to tend all the folks, but there were too many. "Is there anything I can do to help?" I asked. Now, don't get me wrong. I didn't give a hoot about helping Eastham, but I liked most of the folks in this town, and I figured if I could help them, I would.

"Well, if you want to help, why don't you run along over to the saloon. Mr. Simmons and Miss Briscoe are trying to set up some beds so we can move all the patients there."

Now let me tell you, turning that saloon into a hospital was quite a chore. For one thing, Joe didn't help a lick. He just sat behind the bar, scratching his belly and griping about everything we did.

Gladeys was running a broom along the walls, knocking down cobwebs. She stopped, wiping a little gleam of sweat from her brow. "I declare, Mr. Havens, this place is filthy!"

Taking a drink from his bottles, Joe eyed her with a wary look. Belching loudly, he sat the bottle down. "'Course it is. It's a saloon. They ain't supposed to be clean."

If that was true, this here musta been the best saloon in the world. We'd already cleaned an hour, and in about another hour, we'd have the place slicked up enough to call it a pigsty.

Turley slid a chair up beside Gladeys, taking the broom from her hands. "Here, ma'am, you're working way too hard. You sit and rest a spell. I'll do that for you."

I don't reckon Turley really knew how to run a broom because he took a long time looking the thing over, turning it in his hands. What Turley lacked in technique, he made up for in effort, swinging that broom like a man cutting hay. I swear, he was stirring more dirt in the air than he was getting pushed out the door.

Giggling, Gladeys took the broom from his hands. "Thank you for your help, Mr. Simmons, but I can handle the sweeping. Perhaps you could help Teddy set up the cots."

Wheezing like a forge bellows with a hole, Turley came to where I was setting up the cots. "Man, that sweeping is hard work. I don't know how them women do it."

I could only shrug, my brooming experience being mighty lean. We were just getting back to work when Mr. Claude came in. Joe had been leaning back in his chair doing his level-best suck in the bottom of a whiskey bottle when Mr. Claude commenced to breaking tables. Joe let out a roar, and tried to get up, but all he succeeded in doing was tipping over his chair and spilling whiskey everywhere.

Spitting whiskey and clawing at his eyes, Joe came off the floor fighting mad. "What the devil are you doing?" he sputtered, still mad as a drowned rat.

"Making signs," Mr. Claude answered calmly.

"Signs? Signs fer what?"

"The doctor wants signs put up all around outside of town, warning folks away."

"How come you gotta break up my tables. Can't you find some boards someplace else?"

Mr. Claude gave Joe an aloof look. "You know as well as I do, there isn't any spare lumber in this whole town."

Now, Mr. Claude was right. In the last few months, Whiskey City had taken a real licking. It took every spare board left to cover up all the broken windows and doors. The worst of it was, the damage had been done by the townsfolk themselves.

Growling under his breath, Joe returned to his seat behind the bar. Despite Joe Havens's protests we finally turned the saloon into a hospital and started moving all the sick folks in there.

Wiesmulluer was the first one we moved and he griped the whole time. For someone who always acted tough enough to whip the world, Wiesmulluer sure had changed his tune. Now he was sniffling and carrying on like a schoolgirl. Just listening to him was enough to set me to thinking. That disease must be tougher than boot leather and meaner'n an outhouse dog. Anything that could tackle old man Wiesmulluer and Iris at the same time and put them both down was something mighty fierce.

While Eastham and Eddy tried to tend to the sick folks, me and Turley gathered up the signs Mr. Claude made. With the signs tied behind my saddle and Turley riding beside me, I rode slowly out of town. We had ridden more than a mile, and Turley hadn't so much as said a word, which had to be an all-time record for him.

I glanced over at him, just to make sure the old geezer hadn't went and caught the croup like the others. Except for a dopey expression, he looked fine to me. "You feeling all right, Turley?" I asked, pulling my horse away from his, just to be safe. Turley didn't even give a sign that he had heard me. He just kept grinning and bouncing along.

"Turley," I hissed, not wanting to startle the old goat. The way this disease was tying into folks, I had an uneasy feeling that if I startled him he might keel over and die right on the spot. Well, he didn't die; he didn't even move. "Turley!" I repeated, having to scream before he heard me.

He turned his head slowly toward me, grinning like

a champion watermelon eater. "Are you all right?" I asked.

"I'm great," he said, looking even dopier than before. He stretched in the saddle, rubbing his jaw and looking at the sky. "Boy, that Gladeys Briscoe, she sure is quite a woman."

I ran a finger under my collar and shifted in the saddle. "She seems right nice," I agreed, feeling uncomfortable.

"Nice?" Turley brayed, "She's more than nice. Did you see her hair? It shines like moonlight on the water. Have you ever seen anything more purty in your life?"

"We should put a sign right here," I decided, jumping from my horse.

"Yes, sir, I reckon Gladeys is about the purtiest thing I ever did see," Turley mumbled, rubbing his horse's neck and looking off into the purple haze. "Did you see the way she walks?"

"Just hand me the hammer," I growled, wishing he would talk about something else.

Turley passed me the big wooden maul we'd taken from Burdett's blacksmith shop. He didn't get down; he just rambled on, his eyes glazed over like a dirty milk glass.

Trying my best to ignore his ramblings, I placed the sign beside the trail and started to drive it into the hard dirt.

As I drove the stake, I thought about the dead man's daybook, buried in my mine. I knew I should go dig it up, but just the thought of going back to that mine was enough to put a pucker in my drawers.

Leaning on the sign, I took off my hat and wiped the sweat from my forehead on my shirt sleeve. That dead man had family that would be wondering about him. That book might tell me who he was. Clamping my hat back on, I made up my mind. I was going to get that book.

As we rode, Turley yammered away, but I didn't hear a word he said. My mind locked on the memory of that cave-in. My palms were sweating and my stomach jumpy as we rode up to the mine. Pulling my horse to a stop, I stared at what was left of my mine. Just looking at it was enough to give me the chills. It reminded me too much of a grave, which it almost had been.

Shutting my eyes, I screwed up my courage, trying to get the nerve to do what I had to do. Opening my eyes, I started to dismount, determined to do this. All of a sudden, I stopped, one foot still in the stirrup. Somebody had beat us here. Plain as day, I could see where they had dug. Turley and I got down and looked, but it wasn't no use. The daybook was gone!

Chapter Eight

Leaving the mine, Turley and I returned to our job, hammering signs in the ground. We worked until we had the town completely ringed in with them signs. Well, maybe I should say, I kept at the job, 'cause Turley sure wasn't much help. All he did was keep yammering about Gladeys Briscoe.

Truthfully, I always liked Gladeys, even though she was flighty as a whirlybird. I guess I never looked the gal over close enough. I never noticed half the things about her that Turley did.

A fine-looking woman of about thirty-five years, Gladeys had a real nice figure, but to hear Turley, she was a regular Cleopatra.

As we stopped our horses in front of the livery stable, I saw Eastham coming out of Iris's house, toting an armload of papers and such. At the time, I never thought too much about it. How could I? Turley was wearing my ear out. Even as he lay on his back

71

in a pile of feed, he still babbled as I snuck out of the stable. Once outside, I broke into a lumbering run, hoping to get myself hid before the old coot found out I'd scrammed on him.

I ducked into the saloon, figuring to wet my whistle, but it just wasn't meant to be. Gladeys collared me before I made it to the bar. "Sheriff, I do hate to disturb you, but Mr. Wiesmulluer is refusing to take his medicine. Perhaps you could speak with him?" she asked, taking me by the arm and dragging me over to his cot.

Eddy was already there, trying to talk sense into the old man, but for all the good she was doing, she might as well have been talking to the fireplace stove.

"Come on, sir, you gotta take your medicine," I said, not knowing what else to say.

"I don't gotta do nothing," Wiesmulluer said flat out.

"Now, Papa, Hannibal mixed this medicine himself. He said it will make you feel better," Eddy said, trying to coax the old-timer into taking his medicine.

"Bah, what does he know? That tinhorn couldn't tell manure from melons."

I didn't know what to do, but I figured I'd best try to reason with him. "Look, Mr. Wiesmulluer, you said you had cows to tend? Well, if you want to get better, you'd best take this stuff."

"I ain't gonna do it," he said, crossing his arms, his lower lip sticking out about a foot. "And you can't make me."

Well, sir, he was dead wrong about that, 'cause Gladeys had herself a plan. She grabbed onto Wiesmulluer's nose, her hand snapping around his hawk beak like a bear trap. He opened his mouth to beller, but Gladeys was too quick for him. Soon as he opened his trap, she tilted the bottle over his mouth and dumped in a big dose of that medicine. He commenced to kicking and squirming, but he finally had to swallow. He tried to speak, but all that came out was a hoarse sigh.

Gladeys smiled down sweetly at that old man, patting him on the head. "There, that wasn't so bad, now, was it?"

From the look on his face, I'd say Wiesmulluer was of a mind to disagree, but I guess his squawk box wasn't back in working order just yet. He flapped his jaws, but no sound came out.

Still smiling sweetly, Gladeys gathered her bottle and spoon and went to the next cot. Her next victim was Andrews, and you can bet that after seeing what happened to Wiesmulluer, that fat little banker took his medicine without giving any back talk.

"What in the world is that stuff?" I asked, my voice hoarse. I'd never seen anything like that.

Eddy shrugged. "I don't know," she admitted. "It's some stuff Hannibal mixed up, but it seems to be rather potent."

Potent? I'd reckon. "Is it s'posed to cure them or kill them?" I asked as the old man gagged.

Eddy didn't bother answering, she just gathered her stuff and went to the next patient, but I noticed she handled the bottle like it was nitro or something.

Looking down at Wiesmulluer, I waited for the old man to explode, but he just wasn't up to it yet. His eyes were watering, and he looked like a man that had just been clouted between the eyes. Right then and there, I decided to skedaddle before he got his gumption back. Climbing to my feet, I bolted for the door.

When he saw me breaking for the door, Joe went to motioning me over to the bar, his arms flapping like the wings on a big bird. Joe leaned on his bar, looking sour as raw lemons. Fact is, he looked sicker than the folks lying in them cots. "Teddy, I swear, you gotta do something about that doctor," Joe said, looking mad enough to eat nails.

"What's the matter?"

"What's the matter?" Joe screamed.

Eddy looked up from across the room. "Mr. Havens, kindly keep your voice down; we have sick people in here."

Joe glared at her, then wiped his mouth on his shirttail. "I'll tell you what's the matter," he whispered, leaning in close. "That doctor done confiscated all my liquor."

Now, even though Joe kept his voice to a whisper, Eddy heard him. "Mr. Havens," she said, each word sounding like the crack of a pistol shot. "Mr. Havens," she repeated, standing up and walking slowly toward us.

I heard Joe swaller hard as he shrank back. He looked at me with pleading eyes, but if he thought I was gonna help him, he was crazy as a March hare.

Eddy stepped up to the bar, smiling sweetly at poor ol' Joe. "Hannibal has explained to you why it was necessary to confiscate all the alcohol. He told you that alcohol is a very effective treatment for this disease. Now, you wouldn't want to deprive these good folks of the only thing that can ease their suffering."

His face looking like he'd been sucking raw eggs, Joe somehow managed a weak smile. "I guess not."

"Then why do you insist on complaining?" Eddy asked, her voice still soft.

"I'm sorry, Miss Eddy. I was talking out of turn. I know them sick folks need my whiskey. I don't rightly know what I was bellyaching for."

Eddy smiled, patting Joe's hand. "That's all right. I know this epidemic has put a strain on us all, but that's all the more reason why we must pull together. Now, if you and Teddy wish to help out and do your part, please carry in some wood and start a fire in the stove, so I can make some broth.''

I stared open-mouthed at Eddy. The way she came over, I just knew she was gonna peel all the hide off Joe's hind-end. If I had said what he did, I wouldn't have been able to sit down for a month. But instead of letting him have it, she was nice and sweet as can be. I tell you, it was spooky.

From the befuddled look on Joe's face, he felt the same. Not that he said anything. Both of us showed some sense and kept our lips buttoned as we scooted out the back to fetch the wood.

Joe closed the door carefully, then looked both ways before speaking. ''Teddy, I swear, you gotta do something.''

''What do you mean?'' I asked, taking a big step back. I knew good and well what he was going to say, I just didn't want to hear it.

Joe hung his head, kicking the woodpile with his boot. ''Now, don't go getting me wrong, I'd rather take a beating than say a word against Eddy. . . . '' Joe stopped, shifting his feet and wiping his nose on the sleeve of his shirt. ''It's just that that fancy-pants doctor has got her hornswoggled. They think they're running the town. Crimany, Teddy, you gotta put the whoa to them.''

Now if I were to be downright truthful, I agreed with every word Joe just said, but since I was the law, I figured I best keep in the middle of the trail.

''I know Eastham is being pushy, but he's just trying to do what's best for the town,'' I said.

''In a horse's hind-end,'' Joe said bluntly. ''That Eastham just likes throwing his weight around. I don't trust him neither. Anybody that'd steal a man's whiskey ain't no good.''

I frowned, knowing I had to stick up for Eastham, but I didn't like it much. "Give the man a chance. I know he's 'bout as friendly as a cornered wolf, but if he can heal all them folks, I reckon we can put up with him. Don't be forgetting that them folks lying on them cots are friends of yours. You wouldn't want any of them to die, would you?''

Joe done some grumbling and kicked the woodpile several times, but finally, a smile appeared on his face. Well, it was more of a grimace than a smile, but either way it was an improvement over his earlier black expression.

"Naw, I don't reckon." Stooping down, he gathered up an armload of wood. "Although," he said, straightening up, "if that crotchety old bag Iris was to up and die, it wouldn't hurt my feelings any," he added, shaking his head as he went inside.

I bent down to get some wood myself when the door of the outhouse swung slowly open, its hinges creaking like rusty nails. Looking up, I saw Iris standing in the outhouse door.

She was a pathetic-looking sight, dressed in her tattered house robe, her gray hair hanging around her face like a bird's nest after a windstorm. It wasn't all that which made her look so doggone pathetic; it was the look on her tired face. She looked like she just lost her best friend, her dog, and her most prized possession all at the same time. Evidently, she heard what Joe said.

"Iris, I'm sorry," I said, dropping the wood.

A set of tears tracking down her face, she turned back inside, slamming the door behind her. I stared at that closed door, feeling helpless as a duck in the mud. "Iris, please come out. Joe didn't mean anything, he was just shooting off his big mouth,'' I wailed, desperate to say the right thing.

She didn't respond, so I stepped closer to the outhouse. "Iris, you need to be in bed, saving your strength. Now, if you'll open the door, I'll give you a hand getting back inside.''

I leaned my ear against the door, and what I heard like to shocked the life outta me. Iris was crying! Feeling lower than a snake's basement, I pounded my fist into my thigh. All of a sudden, my eyes were burning and I had a lump in my throat the size of a ham-hock. I stammered around, trying to find the words to give her comfort.

Doling out comforting words ain't what I'm good at. My whole life I've always been better at tromping on people's feelings rather than healing them. I was doing my best, but it just wasn't getting the job done.

Then Eddy came outside with that no-good doctor right on her skirt-tails. "Teddy, what are you doing? Where's Iris?''

Relieved to have help, I stepped back, pointing at the outhouse. Shooting me a puzzled look, Eddy stepped up to the outhouse, rapping lightly on the door. "Iris, dear. Are you okay?'' she asked softly. Eddy pressed her ear against the door, and as she listened, the soft expression drained off her face like water off a clay sidehill. "Teddy! She's crying,'' Eddy exclaimed. Lightning bolts flashed in her dark eyes. "What did you say to her?'' Eddy demanded, a dangerous tone in her voice.

I backed up a step, hanging my head and stuffing my hands down into my pockets. "I didn't say nothing,'' I mumbled.

"I bet!'' Eddy snapped. Eddy clenched her fists, placing them on her hips as she glared at me. Finally, she let out an exasperated sigh. "The stock down at the stables need to be tended. Maybe you can do that without causing trouble and upsetting everyone,'' Eddy said, her tone telling me just how disgusted she was.

I turned to go do her bidding when that doctor grabbed me by the arm. ''What did you say to Aunt Iris?'' he demanded, a snarl on his lips.

''Me and Joe was talking. I guess she heard us,'' I replied, studying a patch of ground right in front of my boot.

''I suggest that if you can't say anything nice, you keep your mouth shut,'' Eastham said.

I reckon he was right. Folks had enough troubles and worries without me opening my mouth and adding to them. My hands in my pockets and my head hanging, I headed down the alley, kicking a can as I went. Right then, I felt about as miserable as an anteater with a plugged nose.

Tending to the horses gave me a chance to think, and I began to get sore. That danged Joe. What'd he have to go and open his mouth for? I could get into dutch fast enough by myself. I sure didn't need him helping me along.

Once the horses were fed, I looked around Burdett's shop for something to do. Leland needed to be sealed in his coffin, but I couldn't make myself tackle the job right then. Spying a stack of axes and shovels to be sharpened, I set to it. Turning the pedals that powered the big grinding wheel, it hit me that people in this town were really going to die. I mean, when Eastham first started talking about this disease, he allowed as how it was deadly. But until I saw how ghastly Iris looked, it never soaked in.

All of my life, I never liked Iris and tried to avoid her whenever it was handy. But now, I found myself feeling sorry for her. I found myself wishing there was something I could do for her. I wasn't smart enough to heal her, but maybe I could do something to cheer her up. Then it hit him. Iris dearly loved them flowers of hers. I could go give her flowers a drink of water and maybe tend them a mite. Liking the idea, I dropped the ax I was working on and headed up the street. Now, I had no idea what a body did to flowers, but I figured to sift a little water over them and loosen up the dirt in the beds a little. All at once it occurred to me that I might pick some of them flowers and take them to her.

I stopped dead in the middle of the street, my chest puffing out like a bullfrog. Danged right, that's exactly what I'd do. With a purpose in my mind, I strode up the street.

I was gathering up Iris's water bucket when I happened to glance inside her house. What I saw wasn't right. No, sir, it wasn't right at all.

Chapter Nine

Hunched over Iris's big rolltop desk was that doctor feller Eastham. And he wasn't just sittin' at the desk neither. No sir, he was rifling through Iris's papers like a banker counting money.

Now, nephew or not, I didn't figure Eastham had any business pawing through her stuff. Setting the bucket on the ground, I spat in the dust as my mind mauled the problem over. Hitching up my britches, I jerked down my hat and marched around to the front door.

At the front door, I paused for a second, then kicked the door open. As I stepped into the room, Eastham jumped in his seat, jerking his head up and looking guilty as a fox in a henhouse.

I'll say one thing for Eastham, he recovered quicker than a scat cat, though. In less than two shakes, he wiped that guilty look off his face, replacing it with a high and mighty stare. "See here, just what do you think you are doing?'' he asked, looking down his nose at me.

"I'm doing my job," I answered, pointing to the star pinned on my shirt. "And I might ask you the same question. You got a reason for being here?"

Eastham stood up slowly, raking the papers into a pile as he rose. "If you must know, I'm looking for Aunt Iris's will."

"Her will," I echoed, the businesslike expression slipping off my face as I realized what he said. "She's dead then?" I whispered.

"No, she's still alive, no thanks to you."

"If she ain't dead, what do you want with her will?"

"Aunt Iris is still a very sick woman. She isn't as young as she used to be, and she needs all her strength to fight this frightful disease. She doesn't need to be worrying about what will happen to her things, once she is gone."

"Well, if you ask me, that's a job for Gid," I informed him. "After all, Gid's her husband now. I reckon he should be the one worrying about her papers and such."

Eastham drew himself up, getting all high and mighty on me. "In case you have forgotten, Gid isn't well either. He isn't in any condition to be dealing with this. All I'm trying to do is make it easier on my beloved aunt."

"You're talking like she's as good as dead. You're supposed to be a doctor. Can't you make her well?"

A hard expression crossed Eastham's face as he placed his hands on his hips and glared at me. "As I said, my aunt does not possess the strength of a younger person. It is critical that nothing upset her. She must concentrate all her energies on combating this illness which has stricken her." Eastham raised up to his full height, fussing with his fancy tie and sneering down at me. "I must say, your stunt this afternoon did not help matters. You upset her greatly."

Some of the wind left my sails because I knew what he said was true. "I'm real sorry about that," I mumbled. "We didn't mean any harm."

"Well, you certainly caused harm," Eastham said bluntly, and I felt my ears burn. "Now, I'm a very busy man, so if you will state your business . . ." Eastham stopped short, his expression changed and he looked almost wary. "What are you doing here? Have you been following me?" he demanded.

He tried to keep his voice hard, but couldn't quite pull it off, as an edge of hesitation crept into his tone. He licked his lips and shifted his eyes, unable to meet my gaze. Then it hit me, he was afraid. The good doctor was hiding something.

"Why should I want to foller you around?" I asked, watching his face and trying to figure out just what had put the burr under his saddle.

"How would I know," Eastham replied gruffly. "But I won't tolerate you spying on me," he said, shaking his finger in my face. "Now, if you will excuse me, I have patients to attend to," he said, making a pushing motion with his hands.

While I'm not as smart as some, it didn't take a gold-plated genius to see that for all his blustering, Eastham was terrified at the thought that I might have followed him. Why, I bet his knees were still quaking at the thought.

My mind working like a galloping turtle, I let him herd me out the door. Now, what the devil had he been up to? I wondered as I watched him lock the door. Without so much as a good-bye, Eastham shouldered past me, marching stiff-backed toward the saloon.

My eyes still glued on his back, I walked over to the flowerbed, nearly tripping over the rake. I kicked that rake clean across the yard and gave Eastham's back one last glare. Muttering to myself, I glared after him. Why, I bet the big son of a sheepdog wanted to look and make sure he was gonna get all of Iris's jack after she was gone. I frowned at the ground. Now, that was a likely thought. I wish I'd thought of it earlier and thrown it up in his face.

Making up my mind to keep an eye on Eastham, I scooped up the bucket and trooped around to the pump.

Once my mind got its teeth sunk into the problem, it worried over the problem like a dog with a bone. The whole time I worked, tending Iris's flowers, I tried to figure out what Eastham was up to. Unfortunately, I never came up with any answers, but I managed to put Iris's flowerbed in tip-top condition. Sliding out my hunting knife, I whacked off a couple of them flowers and poked them down in a whiskey bottle. Taking them with me, I trudged up to the saloon.

Pushing through the batwing doors, I saw Iris lying on a cot in the back. Her arms folded across her chest, she simply stared up at the ceiling. Whipping off my hat, I wove between the cots, making my way back to her. "How are you feeling, ma'am?" I asked, easing down on the three-legged stool beside her bed.

Iris's expression didn't even flicker. She just stared at the ceiling, her face looking old as Turley's jokes.

"I brought these flowers," I said, holding out the bottle of flowers. "Well, here they are," I said, placing them beside her. "I tended your garden."

In the next cot, Gid groaned, struggling to sit up.

"Aw, Teddy, what'd you have to go and do that for? All them flowers will probably die now. Everybody knows you couldn't grow hair on a horse."

I wanted to deny what Gid said, but likely he was right. I sure never got anything to grow on my parents' farm. They'd left me a right nice place and I couldn't make it work. Even the weeds died on me.

"Leave the boy alone," Iris said, her voice almost kindly.

Her hand shaking like a dog's tail, Iris reached out and patted my knee. "Thank you for taking care of my garden. And thank you for bringing me the flowers. They look nice. It was kindly of you to think of me."

"Aw, it was nothing. Happy to do it," I said, feeling my eyes burn and my nose run.

Iris smiled, patting my knee some more. "You're a good boy, Teddy. I don't reckon I ever told you, but I always thought you was a fine, upstanding young man."

Well, you coulda knocked me over with a feather, I was that shocked. Never in all my days did I ever hear Iris say anything nice. Squirming on the stool, I glanced around the room and saw everyone watching us. Rubbing my nose, I searched for the right words. "Why, thank you, ma'am. I'm downright honored that you think highly of me," I finally managed to stutter.

Unable to look her in the eye, I looked down at my hands as I mashed my hat. "And I want to tell you, I'm real sorry about what me and Joe said earlier. We didn't mean nothing by it. Joe was just sore over losing his whiskey."

Iris smiled tiredly and squeezed my knee. "I know," she whispered. She picked up the flowers, touching the petals lightly. ''Thank you, Teddy,'' she said, closing her eyes.

Standing up, I tucked the blanket tighter around her, and with a last glance at her shrunken face, I walked away.

''That was a very nice thing to do, Teddy,'' Marie Wiesmulluer said from her cot. ''I'm proud of you.''

''Thank you,'' I said, stopping beside her cot. As I knelt beside her, I saw Mr. Claude sitting beside Mr. Wiesmulluer's bed. The two had their heads together, whispering back and forth like a couple of schoolgirls. At the time, I wondered what they were getting so all-fired chummy about. They'd always been such bitter rivals. Ever since I'd known them, the two of them had been fighting. Over the years they'd had some real battles. It was just in the last few weeks that they'd buried the hatchet—at least to the point where they could be in the same room without breaking into a fuss.

Okay, I reckon I shoulda taken notice to the fact that all of a sudden they were chummier than a couple of chipmunks, but I already had a lot on my mind. I swear, between worrying about all these sick folks and trying to figure out what that doctor was up to, my head was jam-packed. Besides, Mrs. Wiesmulluer was getting all weepy on me. She kept harping on what I did for Iris.

Finally, I could take no more. She'd embarrassed me so much that I reckon even my drawers were turning red. Grabbing my hat, I mumbled my good-byes and skedaddled outta there. I was running like a spooked deer when I busted through them batwing doors, skidding halfway across the street before I got stopped.

Drawing in several deep breaths, I shook my head. Ol' Iris must really think she was dying. I reckon she was pulling out all the stops to make sure she got into heaven. One thing was certain, if she wasn't careful, just the strain of being so nice was going to finish her off. The smile that had grown on my face faded as I recalled just how sick she had looked. She could very well die. Whiskey City wouldn't be the same without her.

Like dust on a windowsill, a somber feeling settled over me. Feeling tired all at once, I sat down in a chair outside the saloon. Tipping back my chair, I looked up at the stars.

"What are you doing?"

I glanced over as Eddy stepped out of the saloon. Now, if I ever needed a reminder why I was gonna marry this young woman, this was it. Framed in the dim light from the saloon, the starlight shining off her dark hair, she looked pretty and dreamy as a late-night vision.

"I was just looking up at the stars and thinking," I said.

"They are beautiful," Eddy said, moving up beside me, laying her hand on my shoulder. "What were you thinking of?"

"The future," I said, rubbing her hand. "What's going to happen to this town if this disease can't be stopped?" I added, liking the creamy softness of her hand.

"Don't worry. Hannibal is a fine doctor. He's doing everything he can. I'm sure everything will be fine."

Now, I didn't care for her bringing up Eastham. Just the mention of his name was enough to spoil my mood. Besides, I never liked the way she said his name, like he was by God and beat all. No, sir, I never cared for that at all.

"That was a very sweet thing you did for Iris."

"You saw that?"

"Yes, I did. Very chivalrous," Eddy said, kissing me on the cheek. "Supper is ready; let's go eat." Eddy took my hand and lead me inside.

Now, I don't rightly know what chivalrous means, but if the reward is a kiss, I figured to be the most chivalrous son of a gun who ever came down the pike. Why, I'd have the stuff pokin' out from me on all sides.

As we walked into the barroom, I could see all the folks that weren't down sick seated around a table in the corner. Eastham sat at the head of the table, like he thought he was the head duck or something.

"I tell you, Doc, you gotta take a look at me," Burdett whined. "My joints are aching something awful."

"I told you, Mr. Burdett, there's nothing wrong with you," Eastham said, an edge of impatience in his voice. "I suggest, if your joints hurt, that you take a walk to loosen them up."

Burdett's face turned redder'n a tomato as he stood there, hands on hips, glaring at the big doctor. "A fat lot you know. A man in my shape ought to be in bed. A lot of walking would likely finish me off," Burdett snarled, then spun on his heels and marched out, shoving past me and Eddy without so much as a word.

Trying our best not to laugh, Eddy and I stepped up to the table, looking the folks over. Aside from Eastham, there was Turley and Gladeys Briscoe, who had their heads together, cackling like a couple of magpies. Mr. Claude sat beside them, a thoughtful expression on the little Frenchman's face. At the far end of the table sat Joe Havens, a flour sack tied around his neck and brandishing a wooden spoon the size of a shovel.

As we came in, Eastham shot to his feet like he

had a wasp in his britches. "Miss Wiesmulluer," he said, bowing at the waist.

Eddy's cheeks turned pink as she beamed at the big doctor. "Sit down. I'll get the food," she said, crossing to the big stove.

She returned, tooting a pot big enough to take a bath in, if a body were so inclined to do such things. Before she hardly had the pot set on the table, Joe leaned over, dunking his bowl in the pot. He brought his bowl out, heaped high and dripping bean juice everywhere.

"Really, Mr. Havens!" Eddy scolded.

Joe had been all set to make a swipe at them beans with that big ol' spoon, but now he looked up, a stupefied look on his face. "Huh?" he asked, scratching the side of his whiskered face with the spoon.

"Just because we are eating this meal in a saloon doesn't mean we must act like animals."

"Huh?" Joe repeated. Judging from the goofed look on his face, he didn't have a clue what she was talking about.

I guess Eddy could see she wasn't getting anywhere. Teaching him manners was like pounding a square nail in a flint rock.

"Are we gonna eat or not?" Joe asked, holding his spoon at the ready.

Eddy forced a smile and even managed a small laugh. "By all means, Mr. Havens, enjoy yourself." An amused smile on her face, Eddy began to fill our bowls.

As she filled Eastham's bowl, he gave her an oily grin. "Why thank you, Eddy. I know if this meal was prepared by your lovely hands, it must be—"

He never got to finish, as Joe let out a howl, spitting beans on the floor. "Dang, Eddy, you ever hear of cooking these beans?'' he sputtered, wrinkling up his nose.

Exchanging worried glances, the rest of us took a cautious bite. Now, to be downright truthful, I reckon them beans were a mite on the raw side, but they weren't no harder than rock candy. I like candy well enough, so I figured I could eat these beans. Besides, I knew well enough to keep my mouth shut.

Turley, on the other hand, well, I guess he'd went all day without a smart-alecky comment and one was just bustin' to get out. He gnawed on them beans like a cow chewing its cud, finally swallowing with a loud gulp. ''You know, if you was to pass that pot over a fire for a spell, it just might help to soften them beans up.''

Her cheeks turning pink, Eddy hung her head. ''I never cooked a pot of beans that big before. I didn't realize it would take so much longer to get them done.''

Seeing the hurt look that sprang to Eddy's face, I was sorely tempted to smack Turley, but since I couldn't reach him, I had to settle for shooting him a dark scowl. ''Just shut up and eat. They ain't gonna hurt you none.''

Turley hooted, slapping the table. ''Now, I don't know about that. Why, a man could chip a tooth on these things,'' he said, banging the table again, ''I bet I could load them up in my shotgun and bag a buffalo.''

Gladeys smiled and patted his hand. ''Now, Turley, it isn't polite to criticize the cook. Unless you want to do the cooking from now on, I suggest you apologize and eat your meal.''

I reckon Turley had more trouble swallering that than he did them crunchy beans, but he done 'er just the same. "I'm sorry, Eddy, I don't reckon there's a thing wrong with these beans."

Evidently, Joe figured the same thing 'cause with a shrug he commenced to shoveling them beans down his neck. I guess, once he got used to them, Joe took a liking to them. I know they disappeared down his throat like water over a falls.

I guess I put away my share, but I know my jaws were sore before I got my belly full. I tell you, eating them things was hard work.

Acting all prissy, Eastham ate his bowl, but he didn't ask for seconds. Mr. Claude didn't even finish his bowl, but he liked to wore them beans out, pushing them around in his bowl the way he did. I don't know if he didn't care for crunchy beans or was just worried about his wife and friends, but he was quiet as can be. Before the rest of us were even half done, he pushed his bowl away and excused himself. I saw him stop, speaking briefly with Wiesmulluer, then the little Frenchman disappeared out the door.

Once we were done eating, Eddy took charge. "Teddy, if you, Turley, and Mr. Havens will clear the table and wash the dishes, we'll see to the others," she said.

"Whadda you mean, clear the table? I ain't done yet!" Joe sputtered, his cheeks packed with beans.

Eastham looked at Joe, wrinkling up his nose. "Where are your manners, sir?" he asked, patting his mouth with his handkerchief. "You've had six bowls already. Don't you know it isn't polite to gorge yourself?"

"Aw, why don't you go soak your head in the hog waller," Joe shot back without taking a break from his eating.

His eyes flashing, Eastham slapped the table, but

he didn't say anything. Instead, he shoved back his chair and stalked away.

Eddy stood up, smiling down at Joe. "Speaking of soaking, Mr. Havens, it wouldn't hurt you to take a bath."

"A bath!" Joe roared, dribbling mush and bean juice down his chin. Apparently, the idea left him speechless, 'cause he just stared up, his mouth hanging open, bean mush spilling out of the corners of his mouth. "A bath?" he repeated, wiping his mouth on his shirttail. "Why in the world would I want to take a bath? Crimany, I just took one firsta last month. And just last week, I got caught out in a rainstorm. Why, I reckon, I'm just about as clean as they come!"

"You reckoned wrong," Eddy told him. "But if you would be so kind as to take another, I would bake a cake just special for you."

"Probably be as hard as these beans," Joe mumbled under his breath. I don't reckon he meant to go for the idea, but the look in Eddy's eyes changed his mind. "Aw, all right, I'll do it. I'll take the danged bath."

"Thank you," Eddy said, turning away.

"Dang woman," Joe muttered. "Why, I never heard tell of taking a bath every month. A body could wear out his skin washing it so much." A scowl on his face, he shouted at Eddy. "I'll do it, but I'm gonna want that cake. A big one!"

As Eddy and Gladeys got ready to help Eastham give the folks their medicine, me and Turley started raking the supper stuff off the table. "If you want any more, you best get it," Turley growled at Joe.

All that talking about cake must have fired up Joe's appetite because he took on another full bowl. While we scrubbed them bowls, I watched over my shoulder as they doled out the medicine. When they came to old man Wiesmulluer, I stopped, turning around to watch the fun.

Scrunching back in his bed, Wiesmulluer pulled the blanket up around him, until only his eyes were showing. "Now, Mr. Wiesmulluer, you must take this," Eastham said, an edge of anger creeping into his voice.

"Get away from me, you quack!"

"I don't have time to argue with you. Now, shut up and take your medicine!" Eastham snapped.

"No, it tastes bad," Wiesmulluer whined, pulling the blanket even tighter around his face.

Eastham's face turned blood red, and he clenched his fists. He started to say something, but Gladeys shoved him out of the way. "Open wide, Mr. Wiesmulluer," she said, holding out her spoon.

Slowly Wiesmulluer lowered his blanket, his face looking like he just bit into a raw onion. "I don't want to," he said, but it sounded kinda meek.

I sure figured he'd put up a better fight, but when Gladeys reached for his nose, his mouth popped right open. Smiling, Gladeys stuck the spoon in his mouth.

Ack!" he sputtered as she pulled out the spoon.

Seeing the fun was over, I started to go back to work but wasn't fast enough. Eddy looked over and saw we wasn't working. "Now, gentlemen, those dishes aren't going to wash themselves," she said. "And don't forget to dry them."

"Yeah, yeah," I muttered as Joe waddled over with his empty bowl and dropped it in the barrel. "You can dry," I told him.

Joe didn't even argue. He just picked up the bowls we'd already washed and wiped them out with his shirttail. After we finished, I stepped outside for a breath of fresh air. Leaning against the building, I sucked in a big gulp of the cool night air.

Boy, I sure would be glad when me and my partner, Bobby Stamper, got our ranch going so I could kiss this job good-bye. For a job that looked dead-dog easy, this sheriffin' business was turning into a real pain in the backside.

To tell the truth, it kinda irked me that Bobby wasn't here. He and his wife Betsy were back east, repaying a debt we owed to an old outlaw and his family. By now, Bobby and Betsy had delivered the money to Luther's family and were having themselves a high old time.

I scuffed the dirt with the worn toe of my boot, wishing Bobby was here. Now, I ain't saying that I missed the crazy devil, but Bobby was a mighty sly man. I had the feeling that it would take a slick feller to deal with a joker like Eastham, and I wasn't sure I was up to the job.

As I moped in the shadows, Eastham and Eddy come out of the saloon. They stood together whispering. Eddy laughed at something he said. All of a sudden, it hit me head on. That low down, double-dealing Eastham was trying to steal my girl!

That's why he'd been so nervous about me following him. A haze flooded my vision. I ground my teeth and clenched my fists. Walking on tiptoes, with my back pressed flat against the wall, I slipped closer, my ears cocked wide open, trying to hear what they said.

Before I knew what was happening, Eastham whipped off his hat, taking Eddy's hand. "Listen, Eddy, the sheriff's not the man for you. You don't want to be stuck for the rest of your life in this rat hole of a town. A beautiful young woman such as yourself should travel, see the world. What I'm asking is, would you marry me?"

Something inside me busted loose, and I charged like a crazed bull. Roaring like a bull moose and pulling my fist back to full cock, I lumbered at him. I was still several feet away when I cut loose with the punch, putting all my might into the lunge.

I reckon if that punch woulda landed, it woulda took Eastham's head clean off. The only problem was, it never landed. Eastham was slippery as a greased pig. He saw the punch coming and ducked. I guess all my bellering had tipped him off.

As he ducked, my fist whistled over his head, smacking into the wall of the saloon. With the sound of snapping and tearing wood, my hand went plumb through the wall, rocking the whole building.

While my hand was stuck, Eastham bobbed up and pasted me right on the nose. Now, I ain't about to admit that he hurt me, but that punch did sting a mite. Roaring like a buffalo stuck in the mud, I hauled off and jerked my hand out of the wall. Well, most of my hand anyway. The bones came out fine, but I sure left most of the hide and some of the meat hanging on that splintered wood.

Paying no mind to that, I set my feet, fixin' to splatter him so hard he'd think he was surrounded. I tell you, it was like I said, that Eastham was a no-account scoundrel. Why, he didn't even give me a chance to paste him. I mean, he'd done had his turn; now it was mine. But like I said, he wasn't playing fair. No, sir, he went and hit me first.

Quick as a wink and before I knew what he was up to, he hauled out his little leather pouch and clouted me alongside the jaw. I don't know what was in that little ol' pouch, but it whumped me with all the force of a runaway buckboard. My eyes frosted over like a horse trough in the dead of winter, and my knees went slack as a couple of wet socks.

My whole body buzzing and seeing four of everything, I staggered and fell to my knees. I guess I saw

Eastham rarin' back for another whack at me, but I couldn't do anything. The gears of my mind just seized up like a rusty pump. The leather bag hit me again like a mule kick. Then my whole body went numb.

Like something from a dream, I saw folks pouring out of the saloon. I heard them jabbering, but couldn't make heads nor tails of what they were saying. I tried to talk, but my tongue felt thick as a flour sack, and the words came out like syrup on a February morning. I was vaguely aware of Turley and Mr. Claude picking me up and carrying me back to my room.

As they carried the sheriff away, Eastham slipped the sand-filled sap into his pocket, a feeling of satisfaction sweeping through him like a prairie fire. None of this showed on his face as he turned to face Eddy. "I'm very sorry that you had to see that, Miss Wiesmulluer, but the sheriff left me very little choice in the matter."

Her feelings jumbled, Eddy lifted her eyes to look into Eastham's handsome face. She had been furious at Teddy for starting a brawl, but as they carried his limp body away, pity quickly replaced the anger. "I've got to go see Teddy," she said.

"I don't think that would be wise," Eastham said, then quickly explained. "Our young sheriff is going to be most embarrassed that you witnessed what just took place. He won't want to face you right now."

Eddy stared down the street and bit her fingernails. She knew that Hannibal was right. She knew that Teddy embarrassed easily. "Maybe you are right," she said hesitantly. "I just hope he's all right."

"He'll be fine," Eastham assured taking Eddy's hand in his. "He'll be a little sore in the morning is all."

"I swear, I don't know what gets into him sometimes," Eddy flared, some of her anger returning now that she knew Teddy was going to be all right.

"He is very impetuous and hotheaded," Eastham said and shook his head sadly. "I don't blame him for fighting for you. I'd take on a legion for a smile from you," Eastham purred, squeezing Eddy's hand ever so softly.

Her cheeks coloring, Eddy smiled hesitantly at the tall doctor. She let him lead her to the bench in front of the saloon where they sat down.

Inside the saloon, Milton Andrews clutched his belly and stared out the window. His cot was next to the window, and he'd had a front-row seat to the fight. Andrews had hoped Teddy would tear Eastham's head off, but the sap the big doctor used turned the fight in his favor. Andrews had seen the sap, and was the only one who was in a position to have seen it.

Feeling sick, his body racked with pain, Andrews let out a groan. The pain in his body, though, was nothing compared to the torment that assaulted his mind.

Milton tore his eyes from the window and forced himself to look at his friends strewn about the barroom like fallen soldiers on a battlefield. A big tear formed in his eye; Milton bit his lip and bitterly cursed himself. His greed had caused this.

For the first time in his life, Milton Andrews took a long hard look at himself and he didn't care for the picture. He realized he was a coward. He should have spoken up and put a stop to this.

Several times, he had tried to summon up the courage to face Eastham, but each time he had failed miserably. Milton had been hoping that Teddy could handle Eastham, but now that hope was dashed and lay shattered in the street. The fight between the two had shown who was the toughest. Milton clutched his aching belly and thought about it. Teddy was a tough young man, but he lacked the deviousness and viciousness to cope with a man like Eastham. Besides, after that beating, Teddy would never have the courage to challenge Eastham again.

Milton pulled the blanket tighter around him and looked out the window at Eastham and Eddy talking. Eastham stood up and bowed to Eddy in a graceful sweeping motion. He took her hand and they exchanged a few words, then Eastham walked away.

His eyes glued on the ceiling, Milton listened to Eastham's boots on the boardwalk, then heard the creak of the batwing doors as the big doctor came into the saloon. Milton clutched his blanket to keep his hands from trembling as he tried to find the courage to do what he knew he had to do.

A shadow fell across his face, and Milton glanced out of the corner of his eye to see Eastham standing beside his cot. Beaming with satisfaction, Eastham dragged a stool up to Milt's cot and sat down. "You look like a man with a lot on his mind," Eastham commented mildly. "You wouldn't by chance be having second thoughts?" he asked, a threat dripping from each whispered word.

Milton couldn't look at the doctor. He continued to stare at the ceiling and swallowed the lump in his throat. "This plague you brought on us is going to kill the whole town."

Eastham chuckled almost soundlessly and shook his head. "No. I just needed to keep everyone in town while my men did their work. I slipped this little potion I picked up in New Orleans in their coffee."

"Potion?" Andrews whispered weakly. "What kind of potion?"

Eastham smiled. "Arsenic. It's a poison—maybe

you've heard of it?'' Eastham paused as Andrews shook his head. ''The arsenic irritates the lining of the stomach and makes a person feel deathly ill. In a week or so, it will pass through their systems and they will be fine. By then the railroad will have their route surveyed and approved and we will control all the right-of-ways.''

Milton turned his head slowly to look at the smiling Eastham. For a second, Milton felt a surge of hope and he clung to it. Maybe the slick doctor wouldn't kill them. As much as he wanted to believe, deep inside, Milton knew better. Milt remembered what happened to poor Leland. ''But what about me? Why did you give me the potion? We are supposed to be partners.''

Eastham chuckled and shook his head. ''You weren't supposed to get it, you picked up the wrong cup. I couldn't very well shout across the room for you not to drink it.'' Still smiling, Eastham leaned in close and grabbed the banker's flabby arm in a painful grip. ''Listen, fat man, all you have to do is lie here for a few more days and you will end up a very rich man. You try and cross me and I'll kill you!''

''Like you did Leland Smith?'' Andrews asked, his hoarse voice sounding tortured.

Eastham stood up in one easy, graceful movement. He stared down at the banker, then smiled. ''Exactly like that.''

Chapter Ten

His mind troubled, Louis Claude rode slowly out of Whiskey City. He wasn't sure he was doing the right thing, but he had let Wiesmulluer talk him into this, and he didn't want to let his sick friend down. The thing that bothered Louis the most was that if this disease was as bad as Eastham claimed, Louis could be helping it spread.

Several times, Louis Claude almost turned his horse around and rode back into town. Only the thought of the stock he and Wiesmulluer had shut up in their barns kept the little Frenchman going. In a few days the animals would begin to suffer from the lack of food and water. In a week, they would start dying. The vision of the animals suffering kept Louis on his course, even though he didn't feel right about the situation. He told himself that the chances of him meeting anybody was next to none. With each passing mile, his discomfort increased.

Locked in his own private world of worry, Louis smelled the smoke, but it took several minutes for the smell to penetrate his thoughts. When it did, Louis jerked his horse to a stop. He raised his head and sniffed the wind, his eyes busy scanning the darkness ahead of him. A look of horror crept onto his face as he saw the dull red glow just over the western horizon. The fire was coming from the Wilson place.

Louis licked his lips and stared at the fire. The Wilsons might need help. Louis spurred his horse, then pulled him up short. He couldn't help the Wilsons without exposing them to this terrible disease. Louis took his hat off, then jammed it back on his head and pounded his fist into his thigh.

He recalled the Wilsons; they were good, God-fearing people. Morse Wilson had worked thirty years for the railroad back east. He and his wife lived in a tiny apartment while they had scrimped, saved, and dreamed of a farm of their own. They'd come to Whiskey City six months ago and made a nice place for themselves. As he recalled how hard they had worked, how much sweat and blood they had put into building it, Louis spurred his horse into motion. If he could help them save their place, he would.

Louis rode bent over his horse's neck, stroking the animal and urging a little more speed from him. Even though he rode hard, Louis could not reach the place in time. By the time he pounded into the yard, a towering blaze engulfed both the house and barn.

A weird, red light from the fire lit the yard. Despite that and the intense heat from the fire, Louis dropped from his horse and rushed frantically around the ruined homestead. He yelled himself hoarse, but he didn't find the Wilsons or their bodies.

He did find a large splash of blood in front of where

the house stood, and despite the heat from the fire, the sight of the blood chilled him to the bone.

A stubborn man, Louis Claude didn't give up now. Time after time, he circled the Wilsons' home, hoping to find some clue as to where the couple might be. Finally he gave up and returned to the spot where he found the blood.

His face and arms scorched from getting too close to the fire, Louis dropped to his knees and stared blindly at the blood. He knelt there as the fire died out and darkness reclaimed the spot where two people had toiled and built a home. The heat from the fire slowly drifted away, and the chill returned to the night air.

Despite the chill, a trickle of sweat rolled down Louis's back and a tremble shook his legs as he rose and stumbled back to his horse. He had to go back to town and tell Teddy about this. Louis swung up on his horse, then took one last look back at the place that had once been a home. A black anger building in him, Louis spun his horse around and slapped the spurs to him.

Louis's mind was busy with thoughts about who could do such a terrible thing. He didn't notice the group of riders that fell in behind him.

Louis Claude wasn't the only troubled man that night. Milton Andrews lay on his cot in the dark saloon, but he did not sleep. He wanted to believe the things Eastham had told him, but no matter how many times he told himself that things would work out all right, Milton could not believe it.

He knew what Eastham's men were doing out there. They were busy burning and killing, and torturing people until they signed over their land.

Big tears rolled down the banker's chubby cheeks.

He'd created this catastrophe and couldn't find a way out. Eastham's beating of Teddy withered Andrews's last hope of help. There was no one who could buck Eastham now.

Milton knew it was not only his friends who would die, but himself as well. Eastham didn't intend to share with anyone. Milton looked around the room and wondered how many Eastham would spare. Not many. Most of them were already lying in their death-beds—which was just the way Eastham wanted it.

After leaving the saloon, Eastham charged straight to his hotel room. Shutting and locking the door behind him, he crossed to the window and drew back the curtains, then opened the window a crack. Keeping a watchful eye out the window, he took a small brown bottle from his coat pocket and began mixing a new batch of medicine. He measured the powder from the bottle carefully. He didn't want to kill anyone—not yet anyway.

Eastham finished his work, then pulled a chair up to the window. Lighting an expensive cigar, he checked his watch, then settled down to wait. A little over an hour passed before Eastham saw the flickering, yellow light just outside of town.

Eastham stood up slowly and pulled a match from his vest pocket. He lit the match on the dresser top, then held it out the window. After a second, Eastham waved the match out and calmly walked out of the room. He took his time, making sure nobody saw him as he picked his way down to the stable. The hour was late, and Eastham didn't expect anyone to be up and around, but this was no time to get sloppy.

By the time he made it to the stable, George and another man were already there, waiting. Startled at the sight of the unexpected visitor, Eastham squinted his eyes and peered through the gloom. "Rupert!" he exclaimed as he recognized the railroad man. "What are you doing here?"

"I came here to find out what happened to my man Crawford," Rupert replied tersely. "Hannibal, have you lost your mind? Was it necessary to kill Crawford and that land clerk Smith?"

Eastham shrugged. "Distasteful as they are, sometimes such things have to be done," he answered, waving off the railroad man's concerns. "Has the board approved the route?"

"Yes, pending the report on the final survey. Since I'm here, I've decided to finish the final survey myself. We don't need any more surprises."

"Good," Eastham said absently, his mind already moving on.

"There is one thing, though," Rupert said, a frown creeping onto his face. "This plague you've created. If the board hears of it, they may want to change the route. Passengers won't be anxious to ride the train through a place where people are getting sick and dying left and right."

Eastham smiled and calmly light another cigar. "Don't worry. In a few days, I am going to personally find a cure for this plague." Eastham teeth flashed as he blew out a cloud of smoke. "Why, I'll be known as a savior around here."

Rupert shifted his feet and stared down at the ground. He jammed his hands down in his pockets and drew a line in the dirt floor of the stable with the toe of his boot. "I'm worried, Hannibal," he said, then forced himself to meet Eastham's hard gaze. "George has been telling me what you've been up to. You can't go around killing folks and burning their places without raising some suspicion. There will be questions asked. When we show up with the deeds to those places, what happens then?"

Eastham laughed and poked the cigar into his mouth. "You worry too much, Rupert," he said, speaking around the cigar. "With this terrible disease sweeping the countryside, folks are wanting to get out of this country before they catch it. Now, since I'm a nice guy and I've always wanted a ranch, I'm having my man George buy these places, just so the folks will have money to make a start someplace else. Of course, once the people move on, we have to burn the buildings just in case they are contaminated."

"And you know nothing of the railroad coming through?" Rupert said, a smile growing on his face as he admired Eastham's cunning and daring.

"Of course not," Eastham said, then looked at George. "Things went well out at the Wilson place?"

George chuckled and nodded. "Easy as fishing," he said assuringly.

"They signed the deed?"

George laughed softly as he dug the deed from his pocket and passed it to the doctor. "That old man was missing a few fingers when he made up his mind, but he decided to sign all right."

"What about the bodies? You made sure nobody will ever find the bodies?" Eastham demanded, his fingers caressing the deed.

"Burned in the fire," George answered. "I even left a couple of the boys out there to keep watch and make sure everything burned."

"Excellent," Eastham replied in clipped tones. He puffed on his cigar, a small smile on his thin lips. "We've almost got control of all the land along the right-of-way. My aunt owns a good-sized piece, but bless her heart, she has left it to me in her will." Eastham looked at the ash on his cigar and shook his head sadly. "The poor dear has put up a good fight, but I don't think she has the strength to go on. I'm afraid the disease is going to get her.''

''What about that bird Wiesmulluer? He owns the biggest chunk of what's left. How are we gonna pry it away from him?'' George worried.

''Already done,'' Eastham assured him confidently. ''When he and his wife succumb to this terrible plague, their daughter will inherit, and as her husband, I shall control it.''

''You are going to marry her?'' George asked, respect in his voice.

''That's the plan,'' Eastham replied. ''She's a pretty young thing and will make a nice diversion for me while we finish our business here. When I'm tired of her, I'll get rid of her.''

''I thought she was going to marry that sheriff fellow,'' Rupert pointed out.

''That's over, I think,'' Eastham said, studying the end of his cigar. He held the cigar in his left hand and rubbed his jaw with the right. ''However, it is too late in the day to be taking chances. I think our young sheriff is going to meet with an accident.'' Eastham shot a hard look at George. ''A permanent one this time.''

George laughed and shook his head. ''I swear, that boy must be part gopher. I never even dreamed he'd get out of that cave-in alive. But don't you worry, I'll make sure this time.''

''No!'' Eastham said sharply. Slowly, his face relaxed and he smiled. ''No, I want you to help Rupert, get that survey done as soon as possible. I'll take care of the sheriff personally.''

As the meeting broke up, Rupert looked back at Eastham. ''What about our partner, Andrews?'' His eyes locked onto Eastham's as their minds met. It was

Rupert who answered his own question. "We don't need him any longer."

The next thing I knew, it was morning, and I was in my own bed. My eyes didn't want to open, and when I finally pried them apart, everything was jumpy and out of kilter. After blinking my eyes to clear the fuzz, I sat up.

Right away, my head commenced to pounding like somebody was trying their dangdest to mash it flat with a maul. Holding my head, I let out a groan. Just moving my jaw was like biting into a lightning sandwich. All in all, I felt like I'd been run over by a herd of hogs.

Doing my best to ignore my pain, I swung out of bed and stumbled over to the dresser and looked into the mirror. I hardly recognized myself. The whole side of my face was swelled up the size of a Halloween pumpkin.

One look at my face, and I knew I wasn't going to be shaving. Not today anyway. After getting dressed, I hesitated. I didn't want to leave this room. I didn't want anybody to see me and I especially didn't want to face Eddy.

I hung my head, recalling how I'd been humiliated. I wanted to throw myself on the bed and stay there but knew the town needed me. With a sigh, I stepped out of the room and lumbered down the stairs, doing my best to hold my aching jaw.

I didn't even make it to the saloon before Eastham jumped me. "We got problems," he said, his voice terse.

Looking him up and down, a resentment built in me. I dearly wanted to take another swipe at him, but my jaw—shoot, the whole side of my face—was still sore as a mashed thumb. Instead of swinging, I bit my tongue and put a rein on my temper. "What do you want?" I asked defiantly.

Drawing himself up to his full height, Eastham looked down his skinny nose at me. "That farmer Claude left town," he said, a challenge in his voice. "He must have slipped out of town sometime in the night."

"You want me to go fetch him?" I asked, waiting as Eastham hesitated. "Aw, there ain't no need in that," I said, my jaw aching with every word. "I'm sure he just ran out to do his chores. He'll be back come evening."

"How do you know that? For all you know, he's left the country. He's one of the few who hasn't caught the disease. Maybe he decided to get out before he did."

I was shaking my head, even before Eastham quit talking. "Mr. Claude wouldn't do that," I said flatly. "He wouldn't run out on his family and friends. Besides, last night, he was talking with Mr. Wiesmulluer. They both got chores that need to be done. I'd bet my bottom dollar they decided to get them done. Once he's finished, Mr. Claude will be back."

"You better hope so. If he comes in contact with anyone, he could pass the infection. That's how the plague spreads."

"He'll be all right," I said with a shrug. "Mr. Claude is a thoughtful man. If he sees anybody, he'll avoid them."

Eastham looked ready to argue, his face thinning down and his thin lips curling into a snarl. Then, all of a sudden, he gave up the argument. I got a weird feeling that he didn't want me to go after Louey and had just argued for show. "If he infects some poor unsuspecting soul, I'm going to hold you personally responsible." He leaned in close and thumped my chest with his bony finger. "You are the sheriff. It's about time you started acting like it. I want you to enforce this quarantine. Nobody else leaves town, you understand?"

With a last glaring look at me, Eastham spun on his heel and marched up the street. I'll tell you one thing, for a doctor, Eastham sure was an unfriendly cuss. Smacking my fist into my palm, I cussed under my breath, wishing all sorts of grief upon the big doctor. If my jaw hadn't still been sore as a boil, I woulda waylaid the big son of a bacon hog right then and there. As it was, I hung my head and settled for mumbling under my breath.

"Has that man Leland been sealed in his casket yet?" Eastham asked, turning back to face me.

"No, there ain't been enough time for me to do it."

"You have plenty of time right now. I suggest you get to the job," Eastham ordered stiffly.

With half a mind to tell Eastham where to go, I turned and trudged away. Where did that big sorehead get off bossing me around? Why, I was the sheriff. I should be the one barking the orders.

Grumbling and griping to myself, I moseyed down to the stable. Burdett wasn't there, which suited me fine. In no mood for company, I stepped up to Leland's body.

After contemplating what to do for a minute, I finally grabbed the front of his coat in one hand and slid my other arm under his legs. Hoisting him off the table, I took a step back and turned. Somehow, my spurs got tangled, and I fell. Leland's body flew from my arms. I tried to hang on to him, but all I did was rip his coat half off.

Looking around to make sure nobody saw what just happened, I grabbed Leland. Poking his arm back into the coat sleeve, my eyes noticed a small brownish stain on the back of his shirt.

"What the devil?" I muttered, bending over to look closer. As I pulled his shirt away from Leland's body, my blood chilled. Leland hadn't died from Eastham's disease. Leland Smith had been knifed in the back!

Chapter Eleven

Milton Andrews heaved his pain-racked body up off his cot. He stood for a second, hand on the cot to steady himself.

"Do you need some help, Mr. Andrews?" Eddy called from the table in the front of the saloon.

Andrews took a few faltering steps, then smiled at Eddy. "Thank you, Eddy, but I believe I can make it."

Walking slowly and stopping often, Milt wove between the cots, making his way toward the back door. As he paused beside Karl Wiesmulluer's bunk, Milt glanced down at the sleeping rancher. It struck him how old and wasted Wiesmulluer's long face appeared. Milt started to move on, then his eyes spotted Karl's pistol belt rolled up on the floor next to the bed. On impulse, Milt reached down and slid the heavy pistol from the holster.

Holding the big Colt out of sight beside his leg,

Milton limped out of the saloon to the outhouse. Shutting and latching the outhouse door behind him, Milt sat down.

He ran his finger along the shiny blue barrel and felt the light coating of oil on the cylinder. Clutching the pistol to his chest, Milt closed his eyes.

His eyes screwed tightly shut, Milt raised his arm slowly and pressed the muzzle of the pistol against his temple. A whimper slipping past his lips, he cocked the gun and put his finger on the trigger.

My face still and cold, I stared at the wound in Leland's back. It struck me as strange that such a small, innocent-looking wound could kill a man.

Whoever stabbed Leland had used a long, slim-bladed knife, like a stiletto. They'd come on him from behind and slid the blade between the ribs and straight into the heart.

Working with care, I slid Leland's shirt back on him, then his coat. Picking him up in my arms, I lowered him gently into the casket. Pounding the coffin with my fist, I wondered who would want to kill this man. Leland had been the nicest man I'd ever known, with a gentle smile for everyone. That smile was gone forever, and I made a promise to find the man that did this.

Turning away, I stalked out of the livery stable just as the stage thundered into town, skidding to a stop in front of the saloon.

Feeling old as the hills, I hurried to catch the driver as he breezed into the saloon. "Josh," I stammered. "What are you doing here?"

"What do you mean?" he asked, clapping me across the shoulders. "This is Wednesday. The stage always comes through on Wednesdays." When we all just stared at him, Josh looked at the ceiling, counting on his fingers. "This is Wednesday, ain't it?"

"Sure it's Wednesday, but didn't you see the signs?" I asked.

"You dang tootin' I seen 'em. They sure look right nice. You folks are fixing this place up like a regular city," Josh said, stepping up to the bar.

"You didn't read them?" Eastham asked.

"Heck no," Josh replied cheerfully. "Never did learn to read, but I can tell time, and it's 'bout time for something wet." He glanced at Joe, who sulked behind the bar. "Pour me something with teeth. It's gonna have to chew through fifty miles of dust."

Eastham grabbed Josh's arm, spinning the staged-river around. "Those signs said for you to keep out of town. We have a plague here," he said testily.

"Plague?" Josh muttered, backing toward the door. "Skip the sauce, Joe, I gotta schedule to keep. Here's your mail," he added, tossing the pouch on the bar.

He turned and started to run for the door, but Eastham grabbed him. "I'm sorry, sir, but you cannot leave."

"Whadda you mean, I can't leave?" Josh bawled, trying to twist out of Eastham's grip, but the big doctor was too strong. "Teddy?" he yelled, looking at me.

"You might as well have that beer, Josh. We can't take a chance on you spreading this disease," I told him, shrugging my shoulders.

"To heck with the beer, I better have a whiskey," Josh decided, finally twisting away from Eastham.

"No whiskey," Joe told him. "Somebody took it," he added, shooting a mean look at Eastham.

"I'm liable to lose my job over this. The stage is supposed to go through no matter what," Josh grumbled.

While Josh had a beer to settle his shaken nerves, I opened the mail pouch, passing out letters to the sick people. A couple of times, Eddy started to speak to me, but each time she stopped. I wanted to talk to her, but I was afraid. She would tell me she wanted to marry Eastham, so I avoided her. I didn't want to talk with her with all these people around, especially that sidewinder Eastham.

I'd just gotten all the mail doled out when I saw Eastham finish his coffee and head outside. "Here's your bag, Josh," I said, draping the mailbag over Josh's head.

"Hey watch it, bigfoot," Josh sputtered, spilling his beer.

I didn't pay him any mind. I had more important matters on my mind. I'd finally worked up my nerve to talk to Eddy. I'd had it in mind to make her come to me first, but as I watched her work, trying to ease the suffering of the sick people, my heart ached to talk to her. I just had to know.

While I wanted to have a word with her, I didn't want Eastham around while we talked. I waited until the big doctor was out the door, then moved quickly, weaving through the cots.

"Eddy, can we talk for a spell?" I asked, mashing my hat in my hands. She looked at me, and for a horrible second I thought she would say no.

Finally, she nodded. "Let's go sit down."

I started to take her hand, but she turned too quickly, walking to the table in the corner. Hurrying to catch up with her, I pulled back her chair for her.

Flashing me a dazzling smile, she slid gracefully into the chair. "Thank you, Teddy," she murmured, her voice soft as a summer breeze.

"You want a cup of coffee?" I asked, stalling.

Now that she was here, I didn't want to ask her about Eastham, afraid to hear her answer.

"No, thank you." She reached out a hand, touching my bruised face. "How's your face? Does it hurt much?"

I shrugged, feeling my face burn. "Naw, it'll be all right, I reckon."

"One of these days, you need to learn to control your temper," she said, and I sensed something different about her today. Usually, she would really rake my backside for pulling a stunt like that. It came to me that the reason she did that was because she cared for me and wanted to make me a better person. The fact that she wasn't mad at me could mean that she didn't care for me as much.

"You're right about that. I guess I'm just a slow learner. Look, Eddy, I wanted to ask you. . . . " My words stuck in my throat.

I shifted in my chair, desperate to find the right words. I didn't want to lose her. All of a sudden, I realized she was the most important thing in the world to me. Running a finger under my collar, I looked around the room. I was looking at the door when Turley burst through it. "Rider comin' in," Turley said, waving his arms.

Eddy smiled, patting my hand. "You go on; we'll talk about this later," she said.

Shooting Turley a mean look, I pushed back my chair. With a last look at Eddy, I followed the old trapper into the street.

Shielding my eyes, I looked down the street. Sure enough, in the distance I could just make out a speck under a small dust cloud. Hitching up my gunbelt, I walked toward the edge of town, with Turley tagging along. By the time we reached the end of the street, we could see there was no rider on the horse.

"That's Claude's horse," Turley said.

I shot a look at the old-timer, but I didn't argue. I couldn't see if it was or not, but I'd learned that Turley had an infuriating habit of being right.

Before long, I knew Turley was indeed right: it was Mr. Claude's horse. Stepping around the warning sign, I walked out to meet the horse.

"Something's wrong," Turley said as I caught up the reins, trying to calm the horse.

"You're right about that. This horse has been rode hard," I agreed, rubbing the animal's lathered neck.

"Never mind that. Look at this," Turley said, and for once, his voice was serious.

Stepping around to the other side of the horse, my eyes followed Turley's pointing finger, and what I saw brought a chill to my bones. There was blood on the saddle. A lot of blood.

Chapter Twelve

Eddy bit her lip as she watched Teddy walk out of the saloon. How tired and worried he looked! Her heart went out to him. She knew Teddy was doing everything he could, but he was out of his depth here.

A sadness on her, Eddy looked away. She frowned as she noticed that Mr. Andrews hadn't made it back from the outhouse. He'd been out there a long time. Rising gracefully, she went to check on him.

At the outhouse door, she stopped. She glanced both ways, her face coloring. She raised her hand to knock, then touched her hair self-consciously. She looked up and down the alley, then took a deep breath and tapped on the door. "Mr. Andrews, are you all right?"

The sound of the knock startled Andrews out of his stupor. He looked disgustedly at the gun still clutched in his fist. He hadn't even had the courage to take the easy way out!

"Mr. Andrews!" he heard Eddy call, urgency sounding in her voice.

"Just a moment," Andrews answered and hurriedly stuffed the gun down in the waistband of his pants. He pulled out the tail of his shirt and let it fall over the gun, concealing the weapon.

Eddy wore a worried frown as he stepped out of the outhouse. "Do you need help getting back inside?" she asked, taking his hand.

"Thank you, Eddy," Milt mumbled, genuinely moved by the concern in her voice. "Walking seems to be most difficult these days," he said softly.

"That's okay. You just lean on me," Eddy said, making an effort to sound cheerful.

For the first time in his life, as he and Eddy struggled inside, Milton Andrews knew the true meaning of friendship. All of his life, Milt had looked at people as a way to make more money.

He glanced down at Eddy's face and saw the tiny bead of perspiration trickle down her cheek. This was a fine young woman, too good for the likes of Eastham.

Milt thought of the gun he carried and knew what he had to do.

Eddy helped him ease into his cot and was pulling the blanket up over him when Eastham stalked up. "Has everyone had their medicine?" he asked, his voice strained.

"Everybody but Mr. Andrews here," Eddy said, flashing a smile down at the banker.

As Eddy and Eastham talked, Milt slid the gun from his belt. Holding the gun under the blanket, he aimed it up at Eastham. Milt wanted to squeeze the trigger. He willed his finger to do it, but could not. Then Eastham turned and walked away and the chance was lost.

Milt blew out a sigh and leaned back into his pillow. He squeezed his eyes shut and clenched his shaking hands into fists. Tears in his eyes and a burning in his belly, Milton Andrews wished he would have finished the job he started in the outhouse.

"That's a lot of blood," I said slowly.

Turley cocked his head, giving me funny look. "No foolin'." Turley spat in the dirt, looking me square in the eye. "A man that loses that much blood, he ain't got much left."

I nodded, knowing the old trapper was likely right. "We're gonna have to find him."

"I'll fetch the horses. You go round up Eastham."

"Whadda we need him for?" I asked, feeling sour.

"If we find Louey, he's liable to need a doctor," Turley answered simply.

Turley was sure enough right, but I didn't like the thought of dragging Eastham along with us. Turley whacked me across the shoulders, a sly smile on his lips. "Besides, you don't want to leave him here alone with your girl. Do you?"

"No," I said. Now, I wasn't nowhere near sure Eddy was still my girl. All the same, I didn't want to leave her here alone with Eastham. Even if she didn't want me, I still cared for her. I didn't want to see her end up with a skunk like Eastham. Leaving Turley at the barn, I hustled to fetch the polecat.

I found him in the saloon and like I figured, he was talking to Eddy. My temper shooting through the roof, I marched right up to them. "We got trouble," I said, grabbing Eastham by the arm. "Let's go."

"Go?" Eastham said, jerking out of my grasp. "Where can we go? We can't leave town."

"Mr. Claude's horse just came in. He wasn't on it," I replied stiffly. "There was a lot of blood on the saddle, so I figure he's hurt bad. Bad enough to need a doctor.''

For a second, the room was dead quiet. It was Wiesmulluer who broke the stillness, his voice sounding like something from the grave as he struggled to set up. "Louey's been hurt?" he croaked, and nodded. "I'm going with you."

"Don't be ridiculous, Mr. Wiesmulluer, you're a very sick man," Eastham said, without bothering to look at the old rancher.

For just a second, Wiesmulluer looked like his old self. "I ain't that sick," he said defiantly. He made it to his feet, but it was plain as day that he was too weak. His legs shook like a hummingbird's wings, and his face turned pale as death, but he wasn't about to give up. That old man was saltier than a drink from the ocean. "Just give me a few minutes to get dressed."

"Get back into bed, Mr. Wiesmulluer," Eastham snapped. "No one is going anywhere."

If he had shoved a firecracker down that old man's britches, Eastham wouldn't have gotten a bigger bang. Dark color shot to Wiesmulluer's face as he stabbed a gnarled finger at the big doctor. "Listen, you smart-mouthed pup. Me and Claude crossed the plains together. That's a friend of mine lying out there; and if you think I'm gonna lie here in this bed while he dies, you're dumber than you look!"

Wiesmulluer challenged Eastham with a stare, but all that shouting took it out of the old man. He staggered and fought for balance, then crashed to the floor. I reached him first, with Eddy right behind me.

"Papa, you must stay in bed. You're never going to get well if you keep this up," Eddy told him while we helped the stubborn old coot back into his cot.

Wheezing and out of breath, Wiesmulluer clutched at my sleeve. "Teddy, promise me you'll find him."

"Don't worry, sir, I'll find him," I promised. I looked Eastham square in the eye. Walking deliberately, I marched right up to him, getting jaw to jaw with the tall doctor. "And you're coming with me."

His eyes wary, Eastham took a step back, holding his hands out in front of him. "Sheriff, consider what you are proposing. We could be endangering countless lives by taking a party of men out there."

"How do you figure that?" I growled.

Eastham shook his head, slowly lowering his hands. "We know so little of this disease. For all we know our presence could infect the animals, and as they migrate they would spread this terrible infection even more. Who knows how far it could spread."

"Hannibal, what are you saying? Surely, you aren't suggesting that we simply forget about Mr. Claude?" Eddy asked. "We can't just abandon him"

"No, although there are other considerations," Eastham said, managing to sound sad as a lost dog. "We must weigh one man's life against the thousands of lives our actions here today could affect." Looking mournful as a drunk with an empty whiskey bottle, Eastham rubbed his hands together, eyeing the crowd. "But I can no more stand by and let a fellow human being die an agonizing death than you folks could. Not while I'm able to do something about it!"

Eastham stood tall, puffing out his chest and smacking his fist in his palm. "What I propose is that I go search for Mr. Claude by myself."

"What?" I said. The sudden change in Eastham's attitude took me by surprise.

"If only one person goes, there's less chance of spreading the disease," Eastham reasoned.

"Why you?" I asked, figuring he just wanted to

hog all the glory of saving Mr. Claude, if the little Frenchman was still alive to be saved.

"It's quite simple, actually," Eastham replied, his tone saying he thought I was the one that was simple. "I am, after all, the doctor. If he's still alive, he's going to need medical attention."

"Oh, yeah," I stammered. "Oh, yeah," I repeated, wiping my nose. "Well I'm the law, and what I say goes," I said defiantly while my mind raced, looking for an argument. "A man would have to be a good tracker to be sure of finding him. Why, I bet you can't track a lick!" I exclaimed, feeling awful proud of myself. I'd show this fancy-pants doctor who was the simple one.

"As it so happens, I am an excellent tracker," Eastham said, pricking my spirits like a pin through a balloon.

"Well, that makes no never mind." I drew my gun and gouged him in the gizzard. "Me and Turley are going with you and that's the end of it."

A fire sparked quickly in Eastham's eyes, but he doused it real fast, smiling sheepishly. "As you said: you are the law. It's your decision."

"Dang right it's my decision, and I done made it," I said, growling and pointing at the door. "Now get going."

Sliding my pistol back down into the holster, I followed Eastham out. Turley was waiting, holding four horses. He handed one set of reins to Eastham, then turned to me. "What the devil took so long?" he asked as Eastham mounted. "I thought I was gonna have to come in and get you."

I paused, one foot in the stirrup. "Him," I said, nodding at Eastham's back. "He kicked up a fuss. Said he wanted to go by hisself."

"That's a hoot," Turley said, swinging aboard his

own horse. "That greenhorn couldn't find water in a well. He'd never find Louey."

"He claims he can track," I said, mounting.

Turley snorted and spat on the ground. "Him? He couldn't foller train tracks."

I shrugged, touching a spur to my horse. We'd find out soon enough. Turley took the lead. The tracks were plain enough, so we rode at a trot, holding the pace for over an hour.

While we rode my mind buzzed, a million thoughts whirling through my brain. We had real trouble here. Leland Smith had been murdered, and now something had happened to Mr. Claude. My mind went over it a thousand times, but for the life of me, I couldn't find no rhyme or reason behind these things.

I wasn't no investigator. I was just a farm boy who'd been given the job of sheriff. The only reason I had the job was that when the town needed a sheriff, I was the only one looking for a job. Now I had a murder to solve, and I wasn't sure I was up to the job.

Through it all, thoughts of Eddy kept flashing through my mind. She was the love of my life and I was losing her. To make matters worse, I didn't know what to do about it.

Turley stopped, taking a pull from his canteen. "Let's rest the horses for a spell," he suggested, passing the water to me.

Turley and I got down to stretch our legs, but Eastham stayed in the saddle, his eyes roving the countryside.

"Looking for something, Doc?" Turley asked innocently.

"I'm watching for people. We must avoid anyone we see at all costs," Eastham replied stiffly. He fidgeted in the saddle, toying with the reins. "Let's get going," he urged, spurring his horse.

Turley looked at me, shrugging. "He seems to be in a powerful hurry," Turley commented, mounting his horse.

"Yeah," I said, helping myself to one last drink before passing the canteen back.

Turley swung the canteen around his saddle horn, waiting for me to mount. "That doc sure seems jumpy, like he was looking for something he didn't want us to see," Turley said.

"Such as?" I asked, looking around, but there just wasn't nothing to see.

"I don't rightly know, but that doctor is jumpy as a cricket in a skillet. I'd say it would behoove us to keep our eyeballs skinned."

"Yeah," I said, taking one last look around as we followed the doctor.

Now, for a feller that was an excellent tracker, Eastham managed to ride right past where the trail took a turn. Turley and I stopped, looking down at the tracks that were plain as a skirt on a sow.

"Hey, Doc, where you going?" Turley asked, nudging me in the ribs. "The trail leads thataway."

His face white and his lips pressed tight, Eastham swung his horse around. "Don't worry about it, Doc, anybody coulda missed the trail," Turley said, looking back over his shoulder at me and winking broadly. Keeping a straight face, Turley clapped Eastham on the back. "I don't reckon you had much experience tracking, comin' from the east and all, but don't you worry none. You just stick with ol' Turley. I'll learn you how to track. Why, in no time you'll be able to foller a fish upstream."

"I have no interest in tracking," Eastham growled.

"Let's just find the injured man and get back to town."

"We can do that," Turley replied cheerfully. I grinned, enjoying seeing Turley tease someone besides me for a change. "Yes, sir, I'm 'bout the best tracker in these parts. Did I ever tell you how I tracked a passel of wild horses clean across the mountains?"

"No, and I don't care to hear it. We're wasting time sitting here talking. A man needs our help," Eastham said impatiently.

"You're right about that, Doc. I can see you're awful worried about poor Louey. Don't you worry, we'll find him," Turley promised, and a few minutes later, we did find Mr. Claude. He lay facedown in the dust, a pool of blood staining the grass around him.

Chapter Thirteen

"Here's your medicine, Mr. Andrews," Eddy said, holding the spoon out. Andrews opened his mouth without thinking, his mind buzzing with other thoughts. "There, that wasn't so bad, was it?" Eddy asked brightly.

Milt looked up, as if noticing her for the first time. "I can't believe it," he said wonderingly.

"Believe what?" Eddy asked as she set the bottle of medicine down and tucked the blanket tighter around him.

"Teddy," Andrews replied, speaking the name almost reverently. "I can't believe it. Teddy wasn't afraid."

"Whatever are you talking about, Mr. Andrews?" Eddy asked, feeling his forehead, thinking maybe he had a fever and was delirious.

Milt grabbed her hand and hugged it to his chest as he smiled up at her. "Teddy wasn't afraid of Eastham. Even after that beating, Teddy wasn't afraid of Eastham.''

"Why would Teddy be afraid of Hannibal? Hannibal has been working night and day to save this town."

Milt grinned and patted Eddy's hand. "Has he?" Milt pulled the pistol from underneath the blanket and passed it up to Eddy. "This belongs to your father. You can return it to him. I won't be needing it."

A puzzled look on her face, Eddy took the weapon and started to walk away. She paused and looked back at the banker, who smiled and rolled onto his side. For a man who was deathly ill, Mr. Andrews looked almost happy.

Milton Andrews was happy. The sight of Teddy bucking up to Eastham thrilled him. It gave him hope. Milt just hoped it would give him the courage to do what he had to.

Eastham dropped off his horse, crossing to Mr. Claude's body. "Is he dead?" I asked, afraid to hear the answer.

"No! He's still alive," Eastham said, sounding shocked. "He's got a bullet in the chest, and I don't know what caused this," Eastham said, touching a bloody gash on the side of Mr. Claude's head.

"Bullet," Turley said, holding two empty .44 shells in his hand.

"Can you save him?" I asked, taking the shell casings and turning them in my hands.

"I don't know," Eastham said, digging in his bag. "He's lost a lot of blood and is very weak. The bullet is still in his chest. I'll have to take it out."

"I wouldn't bother with that," Turley said, prowling around, his eyes on the ground.

Eastham looked up, his face hard. "Do you have any medical training?" he demanded.

"Nope," Turley said, shaking his head. "But I know that a man who's lost as much blood as Louey is in big trouble. You go to digging around for that bullet and you're gonna kill him. I'd say you best plug up them holes and stop the bleeding. In a few days, when he's stronger, you can go get the bullet."

Eastham shook his head stubbornly. "That bullet must come out. It could kill him."

"If it ain't kilt him by now, it ain't gonna," Turley reasoned. "All that blood he's losing is what's gonna kill him."

I had a sneaky feeling Turley was right. Judging from the pool around him, Mr. Claude had lost a barrel of blood. I looked from one to the other, then made up my mind. "Just patch up him up and we'll move into town," I told Eastham. He didn't like it none, but he set to work.

Turley whistled, cocking his finger. Frowning, I crossed over to him. "What's up?" I asked.

"Take a gander at them tracks," Turley said, nodding his head at the ground.

I dropped my eyes, studying the ground. "Four of them," I decided.

"Yep," Turley agreed, squatting down and pointing down the trail. "They came up on Louey from behind. You can see where he tried to shy away from them. Probably warning them about the sickness, but they didn't buy it. They shot him."

"They didn't rob him," I said, following the tracks with my eyes. Then I saw something that made my blood cold. "One of them got down and tried to make sure they finished him off," I said, indicating where one of the killers had stood over the body and fired.

"That's where I found the shells. The way I see it,

the one that shot Louey got down and walked over to here, then shot again. Teddy, they didn't rob him, but they sure tried their level best to make sure he was dead. It's just plain luck he's still alive, he musta moved just as this feller fired.'' Turley rubbed his chin, looking up at me. ''Now, why in the world would anybody want to kill Louey?''

''I don't know, but they sure enough wanted to make sure he was dead, though,'' I said, taking one last look at them tracks, trying to fix them in my mind. ''You know, these tracks look familiar,'' I said, trying to place them.

''You recognize them?'' Turley asked hopefully.

''No. I can't quite place them, but I know I saw them before. I just can't figure out where.''

A fierce look in his eyes, Turley stood up, grabbing my arm and squeezing like a vice. ''Think hard, Teddy, something funny's a-goin' on around here.

''Yeah,'' I agreed, rubbing my arm where he squeezed. ''Let's see how Mr. Claude is.''

For a man that was supposed to be a doctor, Eastham was having a devil of a time getting Mr. Claude's wounds patched and the bleeding stopped. Spitting in disgust, Turley took a small pail from his saddlebag. ''Pack this around the wound, then tie his shirt around it,'' Turley said, tossing the pail to Eastham.

Eastham barely managed to catch the pail before it smacked him in the chops. Shooting a dark look at Turley, he pried the lid off, sniffing the contents cautiously. ''What is this stuff?'' he asked, turning up his nose.

''Pig lard,'' Turley replied. ''I knew you wouldn't know what to bring, so I picked this stuff up at the restaurant.''

While Turley helped Eastham finish getting Mr.

Claude ready, I rigged up a travois. Once they were finished, we eased Claude onto the sling. "I don't like this," Eastham said stiffly. "All this bouncing around is liable to dislodge the bullet. If it moves it could kill him. And I don't trust that lard to keep the bleeding stopped."

"We'll go slow," I said, beginning to think Turley knew more about doctoring than Eastham did.

Despite all of Eastham's dire predictions, we made it into town, and Mr. Claude was still breathing, but he didn't look at all good.

We stopped in front of the saloon, leaving our horses standing in the street. Eddy and Gladeys came out of the saloon to help us, and even Joe lent a hand getting Claude inside and into a cot.

"Is he gonna live, Doc?" Joe asked.

"I don't know. I'm doing all I can," Eastham snapped, using whiskey to clean the gash on Mr. Claude's forehead.

Seeing there was nothing else we could do to help, Turley and I led the horses down to the stable. We worked in silence, which was surprising, as Turley is a talking man.

We had finished pulling the saddles off, and I was forking hay into the mangers before he spoke. "Teddy, there's something fishy going on 'round here," he said, being as serious as I've ever seen him.

I leaned on my pitchfork, nodding my head. "You mean Mr. Claude getting shot?"

"You bet that's what I mean," Turley replied grimly. "And not just that he got shot, but the way it happened. Those men didn't just shoot Louey. They went out of their way trying to make sure he was dead. It's a wonder he ain't."

"I've been thinking on that," I admitted. "What I can't figure out is, why anyone would want to kill Mr.

Claude. Outside of his scraps with Mr. Wiesmulluer, I never heard of him having trouble with anybody.''

Turley chuckled, shaking his head. ''Man, those two had some battles, but don't fool yourself, they weren't never mad, they just liked to scrap.'' Still shaking his head, Turley sat down on a bale of straw. ''The way I see it, there's only three reasons to kill a man: you don't like him, he's got something you want, or he knows something you don't want told.''

''Everybody likes Mr. Claude, and them fellers didn't take anything from him,'' I said slowly, watching Turley. The old trapper pulled a piece of straw from the bale and stuck it in his mouth. ''You think Mr. Claude was shot because somebody thought he knew something? That don't hardly make sense. What could he know?''

''I don't rightly know,'' Turley said, standing up. ''The one thing I do know is we ain't gonna figure nothing out on an empty stomach. Let's mosey over to the saloon and see if they got anything fixed to eat.''

We started walking back to the saloon, my mind working flat out. ''I bet Eastham has something to do with this,'' I decided.

''What makes you say that?'' Turley asked mildly.

''Well, for one thing, he allowed as how he could track. And you saw it, he couldn't track a muddy dog across a white rug.''

Turley laughed. ''That don't mean nothing. When he said he could track, he was just trying to impress that little filly in there,'' Turley replied, pointing in the direction of the saloon. ''Now, I'll admit that as a doctor, he's about as useful as grease on a doorknob, but that doesn't mean much.''

''Maybe he ain't even a doctor. Maybe he's just making this whole thing up.''

Turley reached out and clunked me over the head. "Are your brains plumb froze up, boy?" he asked, standing on his toes and trying to look in my ear. "You forgetting that we got a saloon full of sick folks? No, he ain't making that up."

"Maybe," I admitted sourly. "I still don't trust him."

"I know Eastham gave you a right good whupping and he's trying to steal your girl, but you'll just have to face it, he didn't have anything to do with shooting Louey."

"I don't know about that," I said, doggedly holding onto the notion. "He sure didn't want anybody going after Mr. Claude. And when I told him we were going, he wanted to go by hisself. It seems to me, he didn't want Mr. Claude found. Maybe, because he's the one that shot him."

"What have you been drinking, boy?" Turley asked, cackling loudly. "Everybody's been cooped up here in town. When did he have time to slip out and shoot Louey?"

I didn't say anymore, but I wasn't convinced, not by a long shot. Just thinking about his beady little eyes was enough to convince me that greasy doctor was guilty. Turley had other ideas.

"What I think is that Louey saw something this morning and those men didn't want him to come back to town and tell what he saw."

What Turley said made some sense, but I still couldn't shake the feeling that Eastham was up to something. The way I looked at it, if you were missing cheese and you saw a rat underfoot, then he was a likely suspect.

"What about Leland?" I demanded.

"What about him?"

"Eastham claimed Leland died from the disease, but that ain't so. He was murdered!" I declared.

"Murdered?" Turley mumbled, rubbing the side of his nose. "What makes you say he was murdered?"

"He was stabbed in the back. I saw the wound!" I exclaimed, then explained how I found the wound.

"You think Eastham done it?" Turley asked, and I nodded. "Or are you just sore at him?"

I frowned, staring at the ground and drawing circles in the dirt with my boot. "All right, maybe I don't know if he killed Leland or not, but I'm gonna find out!"

"What you say tomorrow me and you take a little ride and do some scouting?" Turley asked, grinning wickedly.

"What about the quarantine? You know we ain't supposed to leave town," I said doubtfully.

Cocking his head, Turley looked at me, daring me with his smile. "You gonna let that fancy-pants doctor tell you what to do? Just who's running this town anyway?"

"I am!" I thundered.

"Sure you are," Turley said, putting his arm around my shoulders, pulling me toward the saloon. "You're the law in these parts and a man's been shot. It's your job; no, by God it's your duty, to go do some snooping around."

Turley clapped me on the back, hard enough to drive the wind out of my lungs. "Folks around here are depending on you. You don't want to let them down? Shoot no! You're not going to let that doctor push you around. Are you?"

"Heck no!" I yelled. "Matter of fact, I'm going over and tell that tinhorn just the way things are going to be from now on!"

"You dang right you are!" Turley agreed solemnly. "And don't you worry, I'll be right behind you."

By the time we reached the saloon, I was worked into a lather. I stormed into the place, nearly tearing the doors from the building. I screeched to a halt, my jaw set as I looked for Eastham. I saw the skunk leaning against the bar having a cup of coffee.

He glanced up, giving me a snooty look, and that was all it took to set me off. Gritting my teeth, I stomped right up to him. "Me and you are gonna set some things straight," I said with a growl.

Eastham smiled, which only served to infuriate me more. "Of course, Sheriff. What's on your mind?"

"What's on my mind?" I roared, so mad that I clean forgot what I was gonna say.

"Teddy's tired of you throwing your weight around," Turley allowed, shoving me at Eastham.

"Yeah, I'm sick and tired of you trying to boss everyone around," I said, wiping my mouth with the back of my hand. I might have started slow, but once I got rolling, I really got a head of steam built and lit into him like a cur dog. "It's high time you learned who's running things around here," I thundered, pulling the badge from my chest and shoving it in his face. "I'm in charge, and from now on I'm calling all the shots, and I don't want any back talk from you. You got that?"

I could feel my face burning and my heart thumping. I was all keyed up, ready for Eastham to put up a scrap, but he never done it. Plastering an innocent look on his face, Eastham sat his coffee cup on the bar, shaking his head sadly. "Sheriff, I am truly sorry if I have offended you. That certainly wasn't my intention. I have merely offered my services and my opinions in an effort to help."

"Hogwash!" Turley shouted, nudging me. "He's been riding his high horse, making a fool of you."

"That's right!" I declared, poking Eastham in the chest. "From now on, you just concentrate on getting these folks well," I said, gesturing to the sick folks with a sweep of my arm. "You just worry about making them well and leave the running of the town to me."

Eastham's face turned cloudy, and I could see it was a real fight, but he managed to keep a rein on his temper. After a few seconds, he relaxed, but he couldn't quite pull off a smile. "Of course, Sheriff. I am only here to help. If there is anything I can do to help, all you have to do is ask."

"Oh, yeah?" I growled, wishing he would argue with me. "Well, I don't need your help."

"Teddy!" Eddy said, stamping her foot. "You could show some appreciation. After all, Hannibal is doing everything he can to help us. You should be ashamed of yourself and your behavior. It wouldn't hurt for you to apologize to Hannibal."

Before I even had a chance to think of an answer, Turley let out a howl, slapping the side of his face. "Apologize. What's Teddy got to apologize for? If you ask me, it's this greenhorn that needs to say he's sorry."

"He insulted Hannibal!"

"Sheep dip!" Turley said shortly. "If you ask me, calling Eastham a polecat is an insult to skunks."

"In case you haven't noticed, nobody is asking you," Eddy shot right back.

An uneasy silence descended on the saloon. The only one in the place who looked comfortable was Eastham. He leaned casually against the bar, a satisfied look on his clean-shaven face. Sipping his coffee, he seemed happy to let Eddy fight his battles. I think he liked the fact that she was sticking up for him.

He gave me a sly smile, then turned a sad face to the rest of the folks. "I can see my presence is upsetting the sheriff. I'll go and let him cool down."

With that, Eastham slunk out of the saloon while I pawed the ground and snorted through my nose. With Eastham gone, my anger drained out of me, leaving me dog tired.

I was thinking about catching a nap when I saw Andrews waving me over to his cot. I dragged my feet as I slouched over to him. All that shoutin' and fussin' had took the starch right out of me. I was in no mood to hear another of his get-rich schemes.

"How are you feeling, Mr. Andrews?" I asked, dropping onto the stool beside his bed.

"Never mind that," he growled, grabbing me by the arm and pulling me close. "I know what's going on around here!"

Now that grabbed my attention by the horns. I leaned in even closer. "What do you know?"

"I know the railroad is coming through Whiskey City. Eastham is trying to gobble up all the land before the word gets out. That's why he cooked up this phony plague, to keep everybody cooped up in town. His men are out there right now, burning folks out and stealing their land."

"How do you know all of this?"

Andrews squirmed in his bed and pulled the blanket up tight around him. "That's not important. Let's just say that I know. And I know Eastham killed Leland Smith."

"Leland was knifed in the back," I said slowly, my mind rolling over the banker's words. "But why would anybody want to kill Leland? He wasn't a threat to anyone."

"Eastham broke into the land office to steal some deeds. Leland caught him," Andrews said, then looked up at me, his eyes bright with hope. "What are you going to do about all of this?"

Now *there* was a question. "I'll do what needs to be done," I assured him, smiling. "You just rest easy."

Moving to the door, I caught Turley's attention, motioning for him to come outside. "What the matter, now?" he asked.

Looking both ways, I grabbed Turley, dragging him around the corner between the buildings. "I just found something out," I said, then looked around again. "I just found out the railroad is coming!" I said, then repeated what Andrews had told me.

"So the railroad is coming?" Turley mused. He rubbed his chin, looking thoughtfully up at the sky. "And Eastham knows about this?"

"You just bet he does!" I yelled. "I tried to tell you all along we shouldn't trust the big polecat." Pacing back and forth, I smacked my fist into my palm. "Like you said, Mr. Claude saw something, and I'm going to go find out what it was! Did you notice how Louey's face was singed? I reckon he caught them burning someone out. I say we ride out and find out who; then we'd have something on Eastham."

Turley smiled and shook his head. "I got a better idea. How about me and you moseying over to Eastham's room and stirring through his stuff? You never know what we might turn up. We might even find a stiletto knife."

"You mean, just kick in his door and paw through his stuff?" I asked doubtfully. "Somehow, that don't sound legal to me."

" 'Course it's legal," Turley said, clapping me on

the back. "You're the law in these parts. You got a right to know what folks are up to."

"All right. Let's go," I said.

I led the way over to the hotel. When we reached Eastham's room, I was going to try the knob on the chance the door wasn't locked, but Turley never gave me the chance. Slamming his shoulder into the door, he busted it open.

He stood in the middle of the room, rubbing his hands together and smacking his lips. "Let's do some snooping," he said, lighting a match and stepping inside. Holding the match up, he crossed to the lamp on the dresser.

As the light spread slowly through the room, I saw it just lying on the bed. The dead man's daybook! Picking it up, I leafed through the pages. "Look at this, Turley. There's a map and everything."

"Never mind that. Look what I found," Turley said, shaking a stack of papers in my face.

"What're these?" I asked, taking them from him.

"Land deeds. All in Eastham's name. Here's some homestead claims," Turley replied. "Somebody's been filing a lot of claims. My guess is that they're working for Eastham."

I looked at the locations of the claims, comparing them to the line on the map. Every one of the claims fell in line with where the tracks were going to be laid. I picked up a piece of paper and my face turned red as I read it. "Did you see this?" I asked, a hot wave of anger building in me. "It's Iris's will. She just changed it, leaving all her land and her lots here in town to Eastham."

"Let me guess. She owns the lots where they want to build the train station?" Turley asked, pawing through the dresser drawers.

"Yeah," I replied, crumpling the papers as I clenched my fists.

Turley let out a low whistle. "Teddy, take a gander at this," he said.

"What is it? The knife?"

"Nope," Turley said, holding a brown bottle out for me to see. "Arsenic. It's a poison," Turley replied grimly.

"That's how that railroad man died!" I exclaimed, taking the bottle from his fingers.

"Likely," Turley growled. "And likely, that's what's wrong with the folks over at the saloon."

"Let's go get that miserable snake," I thundered, throwing the bottle down on the bed.

Mad as hornets, we threw open the door, ready to storm down to the saloon and string Eastham up. The only problem was we ran bellyfirst into a shotgun. That shotgun was backed up by a hallway full of rough-looking men.

Chapter Fourteen

"You make one peep and it will be your last," a hissing voice said, the very sound of it chilling me like the buzz of a rattler.

I didn't make a sound or move a muscle; I believed what the man said. Not that it mattered—I couldn't have squawked if I'd wanted to. My throat was locked up tighter than a bank vault.

I might not have been able to talk, but Turley sure could. "Hey, bozo, watch where you're poking that thing," he bawled.

"Shut your yap, old man," the leader of the bunch growled, slugging Turley with his shotgun. With a small cry, Turley wilted to the ground and didn't move.

Anger crashed over me, and I doubled up my fist, taking a step toward Turley's attacker. "Hold it, big man," he said, gouging me in the belly with the gun. "Pick him up and carry him over to the jail," he ordered, then turned to his friends. "One of you go get Eastham."

"Sure thing, George," one of them said, and took off on a dead run.

With the shotgun grinding in my back, I carried Turley over to the jail, hoping someone might see me. Unfortunately, the whole town was dark and silent, reminding me of a tomb. A shiver raced up and down my spine. And believe me, that shiver wasn't entirely caused by the cold.

I turned and started to ask what they wanted, but another sharp prod from that shotgun kept me moving. Nobody spoke as we crossed the street. They just kept herding me in the direction of the jail. The inside of the jail was gloomy, but I could make out several more men inside. Grabbing my arm, one of them shoved me into a cell and slammed the door.

Squeaking loudly, the front door opened as I dumped Turley into a bunk. Turning around, I saw Eastham standing in the door, a smug smile on his face. The smile dimmed a bit as he saw Turley lying on the bunk.

"What happened to him?" Eastham demanded.

A tall, lanky man shrugged and grinned. "He gave us a little trouble. He tried to put up a fight and George had to clout him over the head."

"You better not have hit him too hard. We may need him alive," Eastham growled.

"He'll live. I just tapped him," the dark swarthy George assured.

"Good," Eastham said, in clipped tones. Placing his hands on his hips, he glared through the bars, a smug look on his face. "Well, well, Sheriff, I suppose you think you are smart now. Pat yourself on the back. You figured me out." He stepped up to the bars, an ugly smile on his face. "How's your face," he asked, laughing as he slapped my bruised face. Not saying a word, I just glared back at him. Eastham laughed again and stepped back. "Nothing to say, huh?" He studied me for a second, idly rubbing his chin. "That's probably the first smart thing you ever done in your whole life," he said, taking a seat on the corner of the desk.

He took off his hat, tossing it on the desk. Leaning back, he crossed his booted feet, still rubbing his chin. "Yes, sir, you found me out, but what good is it going to do you? You just keep on being quiet and do exactly what I tell you and everything will turn out all right. You cross me, and you will not live to regret it."

The silence following Eastham's threat was loud as any explosion I ever heard. The silence grated on my nerves, and I felt like I had to say something. "You don't scare me," I said defiantly.

Eastham smiled, jumping off the desk. "Well, maybe your feeble mind just hasn't grasped the situation yet," he said, his smile growing as he approached the bars. He flipped his wrist, and a small pistol shot out of his sleeve and into his hand. "I could kill you anytime," he said, pointing the gun at my face.

For a second, there was a wild look in his eyes, and I knew he would pull the trigger. For what seemed like an eternity, he stared at me, his hand trembling slightly. Then he flicked his hand away, the small gun disappearing up his sleeve.

"No, I won't kill you. Not just yet," Eastham said, rubbing his hands together. I could tell he was enjoying this. "Do you know why I decided not to kill you?"

I didn't bother to answer. Truthfully, I didn't trust

myself to speak. I had a feeling that if I opened my mouth, all that would come out was a scream.

At first, Eastham seemed irritated by my silence, but he quickly shrugged it off. "Still not talking? Well, no matter." He sat back down on the desk, looking smug again. "You see, my good sheriff, I simply do not need to kill you. You will cooperate and do everything I say. If you cause trouble, you can start digging graves for your friends over in the saloon."

"The sickness, you caused it," I said accusingly.

Eastham actually laughed. "You must be smarter than you look. The sickness is caused by arsenic. Do you know what arsenic is?"

"It's a poison," I replied pointedly.

For a second, Eastham's face registered surprise, but then he clapped his hands. "Very good, Sheriff." He applauded, being gracious, but then he could afford to be. As he pointed out, he was in command now. "Arsenic, in small doses only makes a person wish they were dead. However, a small increase in the dosage and your new preacher will finally get to finish his funeral service."

"What do you want?" I asked.

Eastham held up a finger, shaking it slightly. "Not just yet," he said, shaking his head. "Now, if you will excuse me, my associates and I have work to do. You and Mr. Simmons just set here and keep quiet. You try to escape or signal your friends, and somebody's going to die."

With that, Eastham blew out the light, and followed by his men, disappeared into the darkness. I didn't move, but my ears sure strained. I could hear muffled voices as they spoke, but couldn't make out the words. Finally, I heard the creak of saddle leather and the sound of hoofbeats.

I heard Eastham's boots thumping on the walk. Then they stopped. "Nighty-night, Sheriff. Sweet dreams," Eastham said with a sarcastic laugh.

Shaking with rage, I heard him walk away. As silence fell on my ears, I knelt beside Turley, raising my hands to touch his face. I could feel the knot already springing up on his forehead. "Turley," I hissed, patting his cheek.

Turley didn't wake up slow like I thought he would. No, sir, he came out of it kicking, swinging, and biting. Mostly biting. "Turley, you crazy old goat. It's me, Teddy," I yelled, jerking my fingers out of harm's way. "You bit my finger!" I exclaimed, looking at my finger in the moonlight. "Turley, I'm bleeding!" I shouted, whacking him across the shoulders.

"Sorry," Turley mumbled, still sounding groggy. "I thought you was one of them." All of a sudden, Turley sat up, his voice becoming stronger. "Who in Cooly's kingdom was they, anyway?" he demanded.

"Beats me," I replied, shaking my stinging fingers. "All I know is they was taking orders from Eastham."

"Eastham? He was here?" Turley repeated, his voice muffled as he worked his jaw back and forth. "Why the devil didn't you just smoke the tinhorn?" he asked, popping his neck.

"Because he had a gun and I didn't! Because I'm in jail!" I roared.

"Oh, yeah," Turley replied, shaking his head.

"Oh, yeah," I growled, surly as a bear. "I tried to tell you he couldn't be trusted, but you wouldn't listen."

"All right, don't get all snooty on me. Besides, that doesn't help us now. We gotta figure out what we're gonna do with the polecat."

"Eastham said if we tried anything, he would start killing the folks in the saloon," I told him.

"You think he would do it?" Turley asked, rubbing his bruised head.

I paced the cell, thinking about it. "Yeah, I think he would do it, all right. In fact, I think he might just up and decide to kill everybody once he's got what he's after."

"What makes you say that?" Turley asked, sounding grim.

"You should have seen his face when he pointed that gun at me. I think he enjoys killing."

"We can't afford just to set here and hope Eastham leaves peaceful once he's got what he's after. We gotta do something," I decided. "When I locked you in here, how did you get out?" I asked, recalling how Turley kept escaping when I locked him up to keep him out of trouble.

"You mean, you never did figure that out?" Turley asked, laughing gleefully.

"No," I snapped. "That's not important now. What's important is that we get out and help our friends."

"What did you have in mind?" Turley asked, turning serious.

"I smiled, just knowing I'd hit on the solution. "It's easy, really," I said and couldn't quite keep the smirk of satisfaction off my face. "I heard Eastham's men ride out of town. That means he's likely over at the saloon, and except for our friends, he's alone. He's gotta sleep sometime, and likely he's asleep right now. We can slip in there and wallop him over the head."

Turley grinned, pounding me on the back. "Dang, Teddy, you're getting smarter every day. Before you know it, you'll be smart as me."

"Yeah," I agreed absently, my mind working hard. "I figure we can make him tell what it's going to take to make the folks well again."

"What if he don't want to tell?"

I shrugged, already having thought of that. "We just haul him over here and wail the tar out of him, till he talks."

Turley smiled, his grin growing from ear to ear. "All right, let's go get the creampuff. I can't wait to get my hands on him."

"First, we gotta get out of here. How did you keep managing that trick?" I asked, practically growling by the time I finished.

Turley snickered and was still *tee-hee*ing as he nudged me in the ribs. "How do you think I did?"

"Quit messing around and tell me," I thundered, grabbing him by the back of the neck and shaking him a mite.

"Yeow! Let go of me, you big oaf," Turley bawled, slapping at my hands. Twisting out of my grip, he backed away, glaring balefully at me. "Dang, Teddy, you like to wrenched my neck plumb off."

"I'm gonna do worse than that if you don't quit foolin' around," I threatened. "Now, hustle up."

"Aw, all right, but you sure are taking all the fun outta this," he complained, crossing to the back of the cell where two bunks were fastened to the wall. Dropping to his belly, he pulled his knife from his boot. Reaching back under the bunk, he pried up a small chunk of the floor.

"How did you know that was there?" I demanded.

"Shoot, boy, I built this jail. Don't you recall?" Turley paused, looking at me as I shrugged. "Well, I did. It was Andrews who wanted the jail, but he wasn't about to get his lily-white hands dirty, and no-

body else was going to take time away from their
work to do it, so they hired me.''

''What possessed you to do this?'' I wondered,
waving at the hole.

For a second, Turley looked at me like I was loco.
''Jumping juleps, boy, ain't you ever been in Indian
country before? You never leave yourself just one
way out. Shoot, not even a rat builds a den with only
one hole.''

''Well, there ain't no way I'm gonna fit through
that hole,'' I protested, already tired of Turley acting
so smart.

''You got a key in that desk, don't you?''

I nodded sullenly, knowing the old coot had out-
foxed me again. ''Just get going,'' I growled, grabbing him by the neck and stuffing him into the hole.

''Hey, leave me alone. I can get along by myself,''
Turley bellowed, reaching back to swat at me.

''Well, get going then.'' Letting go, I sat back,
watching as he commenced to flopping like a fish out
of water. In two shakes, all I could see was his boots,
then they slid out of sight and I was alone. I replaced
the board, then stood up, looking around the jail.

Right before my eyes, a hunk of the floor beneath
the desk begin to rise. Turley slithered up out of the
hole, coughing and spitting dirt. ''Dad-gummed, over-
grown lummox. I got a good notion to leave you in
there,'' he threatened, then tilted his head, pounding
on it as he dug dirt out of his ear.

''Turley!'' I roared.

''All right, just hang onto your bloomers. I'm a-
comin','' he muttered, digging through the desk.
''You still had no call to shove my head down in the
dirt thataway,'' he grumbled, finally coming up with
the key.

I crossed my arms, tapping my foot, while he unlocked the cell door, bellyaching the whole time he worked. Like a little dirt was gonna hurt him.

Finally, he got the door open and I snatched the key from him. "Give me that!" I said, shoving it down in my pocket.

"You got any shootin' irons in this heap?" Turley asked, his eyes roaming the jail.

Now, I said I did, but we turned the place inside out and never found any guns. "What kind of sheriff are you not to keep an extra shooter stashed around the place?"

"I had some. Eastham musta took 'em."

"Why that . . ."

Evidently, Turley was so mad, he couldn't think of the right word to call Eastham, although a few choice ones sprang to my mind.

Cursing bitterly, Turley kicked the desk. "He stole the guns! There just ain't anything in the world lower than a man that would take a body's guns."

"We won't need any guns. Not if we can sneak up on him," I allowed. "If I get my hands on him, I'll wring his neck!"

Turley cocked his head, looking up at me. "You right sure you can handle him? He gave you a good whupping last time."

"He got lucky," I declared. "Besides, he had some kind of leather pouch, and he kept smacking me with it."

"That's called a sap. You got any idea why they call it a sap?" he asked, and I shook my head warily. " 'Cause you have to be a sap to let somebody smack you with it," Turley hooted, slapping me across the back.

Rolling my shoulders, I shoved the old coot away. "Let's just go get the polecat!"

"After you, boss," Turley offered, still smirking.

We slipped out of the building, trying to move quiet. For somebody who was usually working his jaws and making more noise than a circus band, Turley could move quiet as a shadow when he took the notion. Together, we ghosted across the street without a sound.

With Turley leaning over my shoulder, I peeked in the window of the saloon. A lamp rested on the big stove in the center of the room, but it wasn't putting out much light. The corners of the room remained dark, but it didn't matter; I could see Eastham big as life.

He was seated in a chair by the bar. His head was down and he looked to be sleeping. His jacket was off, folded and lying on the bar. That little hideout gun was on top of it. Now, don't go thinking that he was unarmed, 'cause he surely wasn't. No, sir, he had a big ol' Colt strapped around his waist.

My eyes found that six-shooter and locked onto it, staring at it for a long time. Gun or not, I still had this to do. Taking a deep breath, I stood up, having to shove Turley out of the way as I did. Grabbing Turley by the arm, I dragged him around the corner.

"Did you take a gander at that hog-leg?" Turley whispered, and I nodded, swallowing hard. "You still gonna take him?"

I nodded again, really not be able to speak. "Good man," Turley whispered, pounding my back. "You go get him. I'll be right behind you," he added, shoving me in the direction of the door.

I took a slow step, then looked back. "That's a lot of floor to cross. He could wake up anytime."

"Aw, he's sleeping like a baby," Turley assured me, pushing me at the door. "Anyway, he'd likely miss the first shot."

"At that range?" I shouted, then clamped my hand

over my mouth, looking quickly in the window to see if Eastham had woke up. When I saw he hadn't, I blew out a big sigh.

"You think that was loud enough, or do you want a bugle and really announce that we are coming?" Turley grumbled.

"We?" I questioned. "You mean me."

"Quit your squawking and get going."

Frowning, I eased up to the door, stopping to look back at Turley, almost hoping the old-timer would stop me and we could come up with another plan. Unfortunately, Turley had no such notions.

"Shoo!" Turley hissed, flipping his hands at me.

Scowling back at the old goat, I mumbled under my breath. Least he could do was give me a hand. Knowing this wasn't going to happen, I put my hand on the door, ready to push inside. I stopped. I had a sneaky suspicion that door was gonna screech like the devil with a toothache.

Deciding not to chance it, I dropped down to my belly, worming underneath the doors. As I crawled, I kept my eyes glued on Eastham, almost afraid to breathe for fear he would hear me and wake up.

He didn't. I made it under the doors and got to my feet, and he never even stirred. Walking on tiptoes, I started for him, gathering speed as I went. Almost six feet away, I dove.

His eyes snapped open, his hand swooping for his pistol, but it was already too late. His hand was just closing around the butt of his gun when my big fist clobbered him upside the head. We both went sprawling, that chair splintering under us.

I jumped to my feet, ready to smack him again. Now, I don't reckon it's exactly fair to hit a man when he's down, but I wasn't of a mind to stop and lay down the ground rules. Besides, I didn't figure a side-winder like Eastham deserved any breaks.

"Teddy!" I turned to see Eddy jumping out of her cot, her face tight and angry. "Have you lost your mind? What do you think you are doing?" she screamed, rushing at me.

Turley stepped through the door, snatching her around the waist and picking her clear off the floor. "Leave him be, missy, he's doing right," Turley said as I stared at them, my mouth sagging open. "Teddy," Turley said, a hint of urgency in his voice as he gestured with his head.

"Oh, yeah," I mumbled, remembering why we were here. Turning back to Eastham, I saw that the big doctor was on his feet, but his legs were rickety as a cheap table. Doubling up my fist, I wound up, drawing plumb back to my knees. Taking just a second to take aim, I let fly. My fist pasted him right square in the face, and his feet shot out from underneath him like he was standing on a patch of ice. He lit flat on his back, a good two feet away.

Before he even had a chance to think about recovering, I piled into him. I jerked the pistol from his holster, then patted him down. In the top of his fancy boot, I found a stiletto. Holding the knife up for Turley to see, I ground Eastham's head into the floor as I pushed up to my feet.

My chest heaving, I pointed the gun at him, slowly cocking the hammer. I thought about it for a long time and I almost plugged him just because I knew he needed it, but I knew it wasn't right to just shoot a man down cold blood.

Eastham was on his hands and knees now, shaking his head, as a big drop of blood fell from his nose. Slowly he turned his head, looking at me with pure hate in his eyes.

A part of me wanted to squeeze the trigger, but I couldn't do it. Blowing out a big sigh, I eased the hammer down, letting the gun fall to my side.

"That's real good. Now, suppose you just drop that gun," a cold jeering voice said.

A feeling of dread in the pit of my stomach, I slowly turned my head. Standing behind the bar was the swarthy man who'd hit Turley. He grinned, pulling back the hammers on the shotgun he held. "Drop it, or I'll blast the old geezer and the girl," he said, his finger tightening on the trigger.

Chapter Fifteen

I didn't drop the gun. I didn't have to. Eastham struggled to his feet, staggering over and ripping the gun from my fist. He shoved the gun down into his holster, then took a swing at me. I'd been more or less expecting it, but I still didn't manage to duck quick enough. His fist bounced off my forehead. Now, I'd managed to miss most of the force of the blow, but I still fell down, figuring that would be best.

'Course, maybe I was wrong. Maybe I shoulda stayed on my feet and took my licking, 'cause Eastham pulled his gun. His hand—shoot, his whole body—was shaking as he pointed the gun at my face. "Don't you ever . . . I ought to . . ." He stopped, wiping his mouth with the back of his hand. He looked wildly about the room, then his eyes came back to me as he adjusted his grip on his pistol. "If you ever lay a hand on me again," he said, then looked around the room again. "You ever touch me again and I'll kill you!"

You know something, I believed him. Fact is, I wasn't so sure he wouldn't just up and shoot me right on the spot. "Get them over to the jail, George," he ordered.

"The girl too, boss?" George asked.

"Yes, the girl too, and take that fat bartender."

"Me?" Joe asked, slowly rising up from behind the bar. "What did I do?"

"You disgust me. Just be glad I don't kill you," Eastham snapped, then looked at George. "Throw them in the jail and make sure they stay put this time."

Eastham turned to walk away, but now he turned back. "How did you get out?"

I laughed right in his face. "You're not as smart as you think," I taunted, hoping to make him mad so he wouldn't be thinking straight. "I'm the sheriff in this town. Don't you think I just might have a key to the jail?"

I'd wanted to make him mad, and boy did I ever do it! For a second, I thought I might have pushed him too far. His face turned dark and his hand fell to his gun. He stood that way, seemingly frozen, while I held my breath. Just about the time I thought I would explode, he relaxed. He even laughed, rubbing his chin. "You are right about that. We did miss a trick." He smiled at me, holding out his hand. "But I never make the same mistake twice. I'll take that key now."

As Turley groaned, I pulled the key from my pocket, tossing it to Eastham. Cursing bitterly, Turley kicked the bar, turning his back on me.

Eastham held up the key, smiling over it at me. "Check and make sure they don't have any more keys, then lock them up." Eastham slipped the key into his pocket. "On second thought, stay with them. I'll watch these people, and in the morning we'll get what we came for. Even if we have to kill everyone in this godforsaken place to do it."

Eastham turned his back and walked to the bar. He pulled a flask from his jacket and started pouring himself a drink. I wanted to ask him more, but George was gouging me in the back with that greener. "You heard the man, get going," he said, shoving us out the door.

As he herded us over to the jail, I kept looking back, hoping for a chance to make a break. George didn't give me much of a chance, he stayed about ten feet back. At that range, that shotgun would have torn us apart.

He herded the four of us into the cell, slamming the door, then double-checking to make sure the door was locked. Grinning at us, he stepped back, laying the shotgun on the desk. He sat down in the chair, propping his feet up on the desk. Tilting his hat down, he folded his arms across his chest and leaned back.

Joe turned to face us, an angry look on his face. "Teddy, you fool, how come you told him about the key? We coulda used that!"

Me and Turley exchanged small smiles. "They would have found it anyway," I said with a shrug.

"Maybe, maybe not." Joe said sullenly. "But there sure wasn't no sense in volunteering it."

"Shut up back there," George growled, raising his hat to stare at us.

"Well, no sense in fretting about it now. We might as well get some sleep," Turley said, flopping down on one of the bunks.

"Move your danged feet," Joe complained, taking a seat on the bunk. While the two argued about the division of the cot, I led Eddy to the other bunk, helping her get seated.

She had a bewildered look on her face as she looked up at me. "Teddy, what's going on?" she asked, a hint of despair in her tone.

I looked at her face, touching her cheek. "Don't worry, everything is going to be all right," I said assuringly, putting my arm around her.

Holding her tight, I looked at Turley, who sat in the corner of his bunk, leaning back against the wall. He smiled and gave me a small salute.

Tilting his head back, he began to hum in a soft, boring monotone. Joe opened his mouth and looked like he wanted to protest, but I slugged him in the wind. "Shut up!" I hissed.

Choking on a cough, Joe lurched forward, holding his belly. He shot me a nasty look, but he kept quiet, which was all that mattered to me.

It turned out to be a good race to see who would drift off to sleep first, me or George. Turley's rhythmic humming was just about to put me under. I was having to fight just to keep my eyes open when I heard George snort, then begin to snore.

Without moving, I shifted my eyes to Turley. We let George snore for a few minutes; then, still humming, Turley slipped off his bunk. Putting a finger to my lips, I looked at Eddy, then at Joe, making sure they both knew to keep quiet. Moving like I was walking on eggshells, I eased over to Turley. Working together, we pulled up the piece of floor.

Turley started to poke his head in, then looked back at me. "You know, he might wake up, and he's got a gun," he whispered softly.

"Aw, don't worry, he'd likely miss anyway."

Turley chuckled, an almost soundless laugh. "Yeah, I bet," he said, then wormed into the hole.

As soon as he was gone, I covered the hole, then walked to the front of the cell. Putting my hands on the bars, I slowly counted to ten.

"Hey!" I yelled, hearing Eddy squeal and jump in her seat.

George jumped too, snorting loudly as he scrambled to his feet, clawing for his gun. His eyes wide as pie plates, he looked wildly about the room and waved his gun. "What do you want?" he asked when he saw me.

"Go get Eastham, I want to talk to him," I said.

"What do you want with him? He's busy," George said, sliding his gun back into the holster.

"I don't care, go get him right now."

George took a small step toward the cell, pointing a finger at me. "Listen, buster, I ain't about to go get him, so just sit down and shut up before I come in there and smack you around a little."

I could see Turley easing up out of the hole, just as George started to turn back. "You're going to go get him. I know something about what you are looking for," I said, desperate for anything to hold George's attention.

"Yeah, like" what?" George asked, hooking his thumbs in his belt. "Hey, where did the old man go?"

George started to turn around while I stuttered, trying to think of something to say and not coming up with a thing. But then it didn't matter. From his knees, Turley shoved George in the back.

George staggered forward, close enough for me to get my hands on him—well, on his hat anyway. I grabbed his hat on either side of his head and jerked him forward, banging his head and face off the bars. He bounced back as I tightened my hold on his hat, ready to bang him again. With a sigh, George wilted to the floor, leaving me holding his hat.

On his hands and knees, Turley scrambled across the floor, grabbing George's gun and pointing it at him with both hands. After catching his breath, Turley prodded George with the gun a couple of times. "Dang he's colder than a mackerel."

"Never mind that. Get the keys," I urged.

"Hold on to your hosses," Turley mumbled, rolling George across the floor and going through his pockets. "He ain't got no key," Turley declared.

I swore under my breath, remembering that Eastham had the key. "Eastham has got it."

"You know, that's right," Turley said, scratching his head. "Where do you keep your spare?"

"Spare?" I echoed. "What spare? I ain't got no spare."

"No spare!" Turley howled, slapping the side of his face. "What do you mean, no spare? What was you figuring on doing if you ever lost the key?"

"I wasn't figuring on losing it," I growled.

"Well, you done went and lost it," Turley fumed. "Now what are you gonna do?"

To tell the truth, I wasn't rightly sure about that one. I scratched my head, pacing the cell. "I reckon you're gonna have to go out through the tunnel," Turley said.

I was already shaking my head. There just wasn't any way in the world that I was going to fit. "It's not big enough," I said flatly.

"Just think small, you'll fit," Turley assured me.

I bent down beside the bunk, taking off the cover and looking down in the hole. There was just no two ways about it; that hole wasn't big enough for me, or Joe for that matter. What about Eddy? I glanced at her. "You could fit."

Eddy drew up her knees, sliding back in the bunk as far as she could. "Oh no, not me. You are crazy if you think I'm going down in that hole. There's no telling what is down there.''

''There ain't nothing down there, 'cept for a few spiders and such,'' Turley said.

''Spiders,'' Eddy whispered, shrinking back even farther.

''Aw, they won't hurt you none,'' Turley said, with a grin. ''If they get on you, just squish 'em. That's what I do.''

Eddy looked up at me, almost pleading. ''Teddy, I don't want to go down in that hole. Please don't make me.''

She said that like I had ever managed to talk her into anything she didn't want to do. I thought about reminding her of that, but one look at her dark eyes so scared and I melted.

Shrugging, I looked through the bars at Turley. ''Looks like you are just gonna have to go get them keys.''

''Huh?'' Turley mumbled, blinking his eyes and backing away. ''What, just go over there and ask him for them? I'm sure if I ask nice he'll just give them to me,'' Turley said, his tone sarcastic.

''I don't care how you get them, just get that key,'' I said with a growl. ''Wasn't it you that said the mind was a weapon? Although, in your case, I don't think it's fully loaded.''

Dark color shot to Turley's face. ''I could outfox you any day of the week and twice on Sundays!'' he declared.

''Maybe,'' I admitted, keeping my voice innocent-like. ''But could you outfox Eastham?''

Turley's face turned from anger to sullen in less than a heartbeat. ''I reckon I could if I took a notion,'' he said, but nearly as bold as before.

''Good,'' I said cheerfully, clapping my hands together. "Our problems are solved. Now, just slip over there and steal that key."

"If I wanted to, I could do that very thing, I just ain't of a mind to do it right now," Turley said.

"Get in the mind," I bellowed, losing my patience.

Turley frowned rubbing his jaw. He was still thinking it over when George moaned and tried to sit up. "You keep out of this," Turley said, and promptly kicked George in the head. With a small groan, George collapsed back to the floor.

"All right, I'll go nose around and see what I can do," Turley finally decided.

"You might want to tie him up before you leave," I said, pointing to George.

"I ought to just drill him and be done with it," Turley growled. "Where am I going to find any rope?"

"There's some piggin' strings in the desk."

Turley tied George, complaining the whole time he worked. "Teddy, if I get killed doing this, I ain't gonna be happy with you," he said, gathering up the shotgun and ramming George's pistol in his belt.

"Just go do it." I yelled, pointing to the door.

Still grumbling, Turley pushed open the door and disappeared into the night. After he left, I paced the tiny cell, my ears straining to catch any sound that might tell me what was happening, but no matter how hard I strained, I couldn't hear anything but the low moan of the wind. As the seconds wore into minutes, the waiting ground on my nerves. Resigning myself to wait, I sat down on the bunk beside Eddy.

"Teddy, what has happened? What's gotten into Hannibal?" Eddy wailed, her voice sounding lost. "Did you see his face in there? He looked like a crazy man. I almost died. I thought he was going to kill you."

"You and me both," I admitted, not seeing the need to tell her just how scared I had actually been.

"What has gotten into Hannibal? Why is he doing this?" Eddy asked.

"Money. Power," I answered with a shrug. "But I reckon he enjoys it too."

Eddy leaned her head on my shoulder. "Teddy, I'm so sorry," she said, her voice a bare whisper. "Can you ever forgive me?"

Now, you know that after all the grief I'd been through in the past few days, I figured to make her work at earning my forgiveness. That's what I figured, but when it came right down to it, when she put her arms around me, pressed up against me, I caved in like a soggy snowbank. "It's all right. I forgive you," I said, and danged if I wasn't smiling about it.

"Everything has been so upset lately," Eddy said, brushing back a few tears. "Our house burned, and I've been terribly worried about my parents. They've been so sick. All I could think was how they might die like poor Leland."

"Eastham killed him," I said, feeling like a heel. For the first time, I realized just how much she had been through in the past few days. Why, it was no wonder she'd been on edge.

"I misjudged Hannibal terribly," Eddy murmured. "He seemed so polished, so nice. I never dreamed he could be so cruel."

"I told you that doctor fella was no good," Joe declared.

Eddy laughed, patting Joe's shoulder. "You sure did. I should have listened to you."

Joe smiled and hung his head, his face turning red. "I just knew, any man that would steal whiskey couldn't be trusted."

"You were right about that," I agreed absently, my ears straining to catch a sound.

"Teddy, what are we going to do about all this?" Eddy asked.

None of us had an answer to that one, so we lapsed into an uneasy silence. We sat with our hands folded in our laps, avoiding each other's eyes as we waited, our ears cocked for the slightest sound.

"Do you think it was a good idea to send Turley out there by himself? Suppose something happens to him?" Eddy asked in a small voice.

I tried to shrug it off, but I was having the same doubts myself and had no answers to give her. All I could do is take her hand and wait.

Surprisingly, Joe laughed; the sound startled us. "Don't you be worrying about Turley, ma'am," he said, patting Eddy's arm. Joe stood up, moving over to sit on our bunk beside Eddy. "Eastham ain't got a chance against the likes of Turley. Why, that old man is slicker than a greased snake. That doctor ain't half clever enough to pull one over on Turley. Just any time, Turley will come dragging that doctor in by his hair."

As if expecting to see that very thing, we turned our eyes to the door. What we saw was not Turley coming to free us, but George moaning and rolling over.

We exchanged terrified looks. If George woke up, he would sound the alarm, and that would be the end of Turley. Joe and I sprang off the bunks as George sat up.

We raced to the bars, straining to reach through them and silence George, but he was just out of our reach.

I pulled off my boot, taking a swipe at him with it, but still couldn't hit him.

"Shove that boot in his face. That'd put anybody down," Joe grumbled, waving his hand in front of his nose and rubbing his eyes.

Well, maybe it woulda, but I never got the chance to see. George sat up with a dumb expression. Once he realized his hands were tied, he done the worst possible thing. He went to bellering and bawling like a stuck cow.

When George finally shut up, the town became quiet as an open grave. A gunshot shattered the silence so suddenly that it made us all jump. After the first shot, three more sounded, followed by a terrible scream.

Chapter Sixteen

Nobody spoke for a long time after the shots and that horrible scream. "Teddy, who do you think got shot?" Joe whispered.

"I don't know," I answered, wishing he would be quiet so I could listen.

"That sounded like somebody got hurt real bad," Joe pointed out.

"I know, but there ain't anything I can do about it!" I snapped, pounding my fist into my thigh with frustration. I felt sorry about snapping at Joe, and wanted to apologize, but we had bigger problems.

"Where did the old man go?" George demanded.

"I don't know, he just left," I answered.

George had already started working on his bonds with his teeth, now he looked at us. "Leave? How could he leave? He was in jail."

In no mood to help him, I only smiled and shrugged. "Well, as soon as I get loose, you'll talk soon enough!'' George threatened, returning to his work.

"I doubt if there is anything you can do to make me talk,'' I said, quietly confident.

George looked up at me, smiling around the knot in his mouth. "We'll see about that.''

He went to work on them knots with renewed energy. It looked like he was close to freeing himself when Turley burst into the jail. Out of breath, Turley skidded to a halt, bending over as he tried to catch his breath.

We tried to warn him, but with all three of us talking at the same time, he couldn't understand what we were trying to say. Finally he followed our pointing fingers, just as George jerked his hands free.

Without any undo haste, Turley hauled out his pistol and plunked George on the head. "Eastham got away!'' Turley shouted as George melted back to the floor.

"Never mind that. Did you get the key?'' I demanded, shaking the bars on the door.

"Great gravy, are you deaf, boy? I just told you he got away!'' Turley yelled back as I cursed and kicked the bars. "I tell you, the lead was flying every which way. Why, I was lucky not to get myself ventilated!''

"Well, you sure took your sweet time getting back,'' I griped.

Turley smiled smugly. "I had things to take care of.''

"Things?'' I roared. "What kind of things? What could have been more important than getting us outta jail?''

"Wiesmulluer's old mutt came limping into town,'' Turley said with a shrug. "I had to tend him a mite.''

Eddy stepped to the bars, her hands white as she

gripped them. "Mike? He's not dead?" she whispered.

Turley chuckled and waved a hand. "Naw. He's been shot in the hind-end, but with ol' doc Turley around he ain't in any danger. I stowed him in the barn till I get a chance to tend him a little better."

Still grumbling under my breath, I looked around the cell. "Never mind the dog. We gotta get out of here," I said, a feeling of desperation creeping up on me. "Eastham will get his men and be right back." I grabbed the bars, looking Turley right in the eye. "You've got to get this door open."

"Just how do you propose I do that?" Turley asked belligerently. "It ain't like I got a magic wand."

"I don't know how you're going to do it, but it's got to be done," I said, pacing the cell. "I wish Bobby was here. He could open that door in a heartbeat," I said, remembering my partner had once been a world-class bank robber.

All of a sudden, Turley's face lit up, and he snapped his fingers. "I got myself an idea!" he yelled, already sprinting for the door.

"Turley, pull in your reins." I yelled, not liking the look in his eyes. "Just what do you have in mind?"

"Don't you fret, boy. I'll have you out of there in two shakes."

"Turley!" I shouted at his retreating back. He didn't turn or even slow down, he just laughed merrily, waving his hand over his head. "Turley!" I shouted again, but this time I was talking to a closed door.

"What's the matter? Can't he get us out?" Eddy asked.

"I don't know," I replied, and all of a sudden, I was more worried about what Turley might do than

Eastham. Judging from the stunts Turley had pulled in the past, there was no telling what he might try.

We didn't have to wait long before Turley's face appeared at the barred cell window. "Watch yourselves," he cackled, then disappeared. In just a second, his face was back at the window. "You might want to tuck in your heads and take some cover," he advised, grinning madly.

"Turley, you just hold your horses," I shouted, rushing to the window. "Just what are you going to do?"

For an answer, Turley grinned and held up a stick of dynamite. I opened my mouth to forbid him, but then I saw, the fuse was lit!

"Eddy, Joe, get under the bunks!" I screamed as I scrambled across the room, my boots slipping on the slick floor. Finally, my boots found some purchase, and I dove headfirst under the bunk. I wrapped my arms around Eddy, trying to shield her with my body as I waited for the bomb to go off. The wait wasn't a long one.

That stick of powder went off like a clap of thunder, dang near blowing my ears off my head. I hadn't even started to recover from that when I felt a searing pain in my backside. I swear, it felt like somebody slapped a red-hot skillet across my hind-end.

Bellering like a bull moose, I snapped up straight. Or rather I tried to, the bunk above me putting the whoa to that in a painful way.

Screaming again, I flopped back down, trying to decide whether to hold my smarting head or my blistered backside. I was still rasslin' with the dilemma when Eddy socked me in the ribs.

"Get off me, Teddy. You're smothering me!"

"Sorry," I mumbled, scooting out from under the

bunk. "Are you all right?" I asked, fearing she might have been hurt.

"I'm fine . . . I think," Eddy said, her voice a mite shaky.

"Whoa, Teddy!" Turley yelled, crawling through the gaping hole in the wall.

"What is it?" I snapped, helping Eddy up.

"Your saddle shiner is on fire," Turley said, and fell to the floor, rolling back and forth as he laughed like a crazy man.

"Huh?" I muttered, twisting around to look at my backside. Sure enough, a thin trail of smoke drifted away from the seat of my britches. Yelping like a kicked dog, I jumped in the air, slapping at my rear end.

After a few minutes of slapping, I managed to smother the fire, but that's when I found the splinters. Well, actually, they were a sight bigger than splinters. Well, actually, they were a sight bigger than splinters. I reckon a couple of them were about the size of hoe handles.

The next few minutes I spent bent over a bunk while Turley dug splinters out of my hind end. "Turley, you crazy old goat, you might have killed us all!" I shouted, getting angry at what he'd done.

"Aw, quit your sniffling. I got you out. That's what you wanted, wasn't it?" Turley said, yanking out a splinter.

"Just hurry up," I growled, twisting around to see what he was doing.

"There, that's the last of them," Turley said, stepping back to admire his handiwork. "Not a bad job, if I do say so myself."

"Never mind that, we got work to do," I said, jerking my britches over my backside, which by now felt like a burnt biscuit. Knowing we might not have a lot of time, we hurried over to the saloon. Standing at the bar, I looked out at the sick faces and tried to work up the gumption to tell them what they had to know. Finally, I screwed my courage up and told them about the disease.

"You mean, there's no plague?" Wiesmulluer demanded, holding his belly as he sat up.

I shook my head. "No, there's no disease, there never was. All that's wrong with you is that Eastham poisoned you."

Everybody commenced to screeching and bellering at the same time. I tried to calm them down, but they weren't listening to me. It was Wiesmulluer's bellering voice that finally shut them up. "Quit your yapping," Wiesmulluer growled. "Is there a cure for this poison we took?"

I glanced at Turley, who shrugged and turned away. "If there is, we don't know about it," I said heavily.

"You mean, we are all going to die?" Gid asked, his voice small.

Turley snorted, waving away their concerns. "Aw, heck no, nobody's going to die. Not while ol' doc Turley is around."

Now, if you ever want to start a full-fledged panic, just tell a room full of sick people that you're going to let Turley do some doctoring on them. I swear, the news almost put a couple of them away.

"You stay away from me, you drunken fool," Gid screamed, his voice shrill as a baby's. "Teddy, keep him away from me!"

"Now, don't you fret," Turley said with a grin as he patted Andrews on the head. "The way I see it, we got to get that poison outta you, and as my grandma always used to say, there ain't no better way to clean a feller out than a good dose of castor oil."

"Castor oil?" Wiesmulluer grumbled, wrinkling up his nose. "I'd rather be sick."

Turley paid him no mind. Looking happy as a lark, he turned to Eddy and Gladeys. "You girls go through every house in town and bring back all the castor oil you can find," he said, rubbing his hands together. "We'll have these folks back on their feet in no time."

"If you find any guns, bring them back too," I said.

"Oh, yeah, if you happen across any shooting irons, you might drag them over here," Turley said offhand, then got down to business. "Once you get all the oil rounded up, mix it together, then divide it up between them and make them drink it. You be sure to watch close and make sure nobody cheats."

While the girls rounded up the castor oil, Turley, Joe, Burdett, Preacher Tom, Josh, and I made arrangements to greet our callers. Burdett and Joe griped, complaining that Eastham probably wouldn't be back, but I knew he would. There was too much at stake. A small fortune. Eastham wouldn't let it pass without putting up a scrap.

I also knew that Eastham's only chance to get control of the land before the railroad came through was to kill everybody.

We had to stop him, I just didn't know how we were going to do the job. We were pitifully few to go up against his men. To top it off, we found ourselves a mite shy of weapons. All we had was the shotgun and pistol we took from George, who was tied up over at the jail.

Six unarmed men against a gang of ruthless killers. We'd be lucky if any of us lived to see another sunset.

Chapter Seventeen

We weren't as ready as I would have liked, but Eastham was calling the shots. He could pick and choose his time, and we just had to be ready. Evidently, he figured with half the town down sick and all the guns in town confiscated, he wouldn't have any trouble, because he rode right into town bold as brass. He didn't come alone, neither. He brought a whole raft of fellers with him.

They were a mile away when we spotted them, riding under an umbrella of dust. In the distance, they looked tall as oak trees. A party of grim men, intent on finishing a job.

"If I had my rifle, I'd plug that Eastham right here and now," Turley growled as they drew steadily closer.

"You'd likely miss," I croaked, trying to make a joke and failing miserably. "You think this plan is going to work?"

I don't know how he pulled it off, but Turley actually grinned. "Sure, it'll work. It's a great plan."

"Oh, yeah, it's a great plan," Joe Havens grumbled. "And it just might work, providing half them fellers gets struck by lightning in the next minute."

Despite the tension in the air, the remark struck us all as funny. As the laughter died away, we shared a quiet moment before everyone slipped down to their positions. I watched them go, friends of mine, and wondered if I would ever see any of them again.

I looked down at Eddy, who crouched behind the false wall of the saloon. I touched her shoulder, then turned my attention to the street.

"Teddy, I'm scared."

I looked down at her, wanting to tell her everything was going to be all right, but I didn't really believe it myself. "I know, I'm scared to," I said.

I stood tall on the roof of the saloon, watching as Eastham and his men rode up the street. Eastham rode in the lead, his face cold and still.

He stopped directly in front of the saloon, his men fanning out around him. Placing his hands on that fancy saddle horn, he looked up at me.

"Sheriff Cooper, how nice to see you again," he said, sporting a big smile.

"I could do without it," I growled.

Eastham smiled again. "If you wish to be rid of me it's really quite simple. Have all your people sign the land deeds and you can all leave this town."

"No. That land is all these people have, and I'm not about to let you take it from them," I said quietly.

Eastham laughed, slapping his thigh with a fancy riding crop. "Look at my men," he said, gesturing to his men with the crop. "There isn't any way you can stop us. If you sign now, I'll let everyone live. Otherwise, I'll kill everyone and burn this town around your ears!''

I saw Turley poke his head out from around the corner of the bank, and knew he was ready. Moving my leg slightly, I bumped Eddy's shoulder.

As Eddy lit the fuse on our last stick of dynamite, Turley edged his horse out in the street. Eddy flipped the dynamite over the wall. For a split second, Eastham's men stared at that glittering stick, shock and disbelief written on their faces. One of them finally got his screecher to working and let out a scream, slapping the spurs to his horse, and the rest of them scattered like a flock of quail.

As the men scrambled for whatever cover they could find, Turley dropped a rope around the neck of one of Eastham's men. Whooping, Turley spurred his horse, dragging the man kicking and screaming between the buildings. So busy was I watching the action, I clean forgot to duck.

The force of the blast threw me back a good ten feet. Flying through the air, I saw the blast empty a few saddles, throwing one man through the front window of the saloon.

A glimpse was all I got before I hit flat on my back. Unfortunately, the roof of the saloon was built with the same care as the rest of the town and didn't hold my weight. Screaming wildly, I crashed through the roof, hitting the floor with a solid thump.

My eyes swimming, I sat up, holding my head. Across the room, I saw the man who'd came through the window trying to get up, his eyes glazed over like mine. He never got a chance to recover.

Screaming like a charging warrior, Gladeys Briscoe lit into him with a broomstick. She took a ten-yard run at that poor devil, and when she cut loose with her swing, she had a big head of steam behind her. It sounded like a pistol shot when the broom handle smacked across the man's face, leaving a bright red welt. Seeing that he was taken care of, I jumped to my feet, intent on joining the fight outside.

Covering his head with his hands, the man crawled frantically across the floor, begging for mercy. He managed to scramble to his feet and make a break for the door. He mighta made it outside, but I beat him to the door.

Now, this man was a killer, maybe even worse than a killer, but nobody deserved the whupping he was taking from Gladeys. It ran in my mind to show some mercy and let him get outside where there was only bullets to bother with. Yeah, I though about showing mercy, but this here was war.

I grabbed him around the neck, ripping his pistol loose from his belt. Placing my hand in his face, I shoved him back where Gladeys was waiting. She smacked right him across the nose, dropping him in his tracks.

Gripping the pistol, I ducked outside, my eyes searching the street for Eastham. The street was a jumbled mass of confusion. Using the guns we took from George, Josh and Joe were shooting from the top of the hotel. Turley had gotten a gun from the man he roped and was pouring it to the raiders. Even Eddy was helping out, throwing horseshoes from the top of the saloon. Like mice in a barrel, the raiders scurried around, looking desperately for any kind of cover.

Four of the raiders had gotten a bellyful and tried to make a break for it, whipping their horses as they tore down the street. Sweeping past the stable, they ran full tilt into a nasty surprise. Preacher Tom and Burdett jerked a rope tight across the street.

That rope knocked them fellers out of the saddle

like they'd been hit by cannonballs. Preacher Tom and Burdett snatched up a couple of wooden mallets and waded into them.

A tall man careened toward me, dodging bullets from Turley's gun. The man was looking back and didn't see me. As he dashed past me, I took a mighty swipe at him.

I'd clean forgot about the gun in my fist, but the barrel of that gun smacked him right above the eye, and believe me, it sure did the job I intended. His feet shot out from under him, and he lit right on his head. He rolled over once, then didn't move.

I gouged him with the toe of my boot, but the fallen man didn't move. This one wouldn't be causing any mischief for a spell.

I straightened up, when *whack!*—a bullet smacked into the wall beside my head, showering me with splinters. Snapping my pistol up, I glanced wildly about. "Whoa, Teddy, it's me!" Turley yelled, ducking his head.

Growling, I lowered my gun. That crazy old geezer had durn near shot me! "Sorry, Teddy!" Turley called, but from the grin spreading across his face, he didn't look very sorry. "I almost didn't recognize you. How'd you get down there anyway?"

I started to answer, but then I saw Eastham. I reckon he had seen enough 'cause he was sneaking down the street like the lowly dog he was.

Snarling, I gripped my pistol, lunging after him. My eyes glued to him, I pumped my arms, running flat out. Eastham saw me chasing him and turned and scooted behind Iris's house.

Running for all I was worth, I lumbered up the street in hot pursuit. A man dove out of the shadows, his shoulder smacking me in the chest. His weight bowled us both over, knocking the pistol from my hand.

Forgetting about the gun, I lunged to my feet. Grabbing my attacker by the ears, I broke into a run, dragging him behind me. Skewing off to the side, I rammed the raider head first into Iris's house. I heard his neck pop a bit as his head crashed through the wall, going in plumb up to his shoulders.

Giving him a last kick in the britches, I took after Eastham. Out of breath, I skidded to a halt in the alley, looking in both directions for that greasy doctor. He was running down the alley just behind the saloon.

"Eastham!" I shouted, wanting to settle things once and for all.

Instead of stopping and having it out like men, Eastham twisted around, snapping a shot at me. Throwing my hands over my head, I dove to the ground for cover.

I guess it dawned on Eastham that I wasn't armed because he slid to a halt. His teeth showing in a wolfish grin, he turned slowly, bringing his gun up.

I glanced about the alley for something to use as a weapon, or better yet something to hide behind, but that alley was bare as a baby's backside.

Likely, he woulda salted me away, but Turley's express treatment picked that second to take a hold.

The back door of the saloon flew open, knocking Eastham for a loop. Before Eastham had a chance to recover, a whole herd of folks poured outta the saloon, trampling him in the dust.

Now, I don't know if Turley's cure was working, but it sure got them folks up and moving. They busted out of that saloon like a cavalry charge. I can say one thing for sure, if you're ever going to give a dozen or so people a dose of castor oil, make sure you have more than a two-seater outhouse.

While they battled to see who got in, Eastham staggered to his feet. Shaking his head, the big doctor glanced about for his gun. His eyes widened as he spotted the weapon. He bent down to get it when I slammed into him. We crashed into the saloon, bouncing back a good five feet. Eastham cursed wildly as we tangled our feet and hit the ground.

Trying to catch my breath, I scrambled to my feet while Eastham rose slowly. "You want another beating?" Eastham asked, smiling, as he cracked his knuckles.

You know, I wasn't afraid anymore. As a matter of fact, I welcomed this chance to put a few dents in his skull.

Eastham circled to the right, rolling his shoulders. "I'm going to enjoy this," he said, clenching his fists.

In the street, I could here the sounds of the battle still raging. Ignoring that, I concentrated all my attention on Eastham. Setting his feet, the doctor charged, sending a long looping punch at my head.

Ducking inside the punch, I grabbed Eastham around the waist. Hauling him up off the ground, I ran forward, ramming his back into the wall of the saloon.

As we bounced off the wall, I elbowed him in the ear, feeling blood on my arm. Howling in pain, Eastham tangled his legs in mine, tripping both of us. Now, for a slick, citified doctor, Eastham sure knew a lot about dirty fighting. As we rolled on the ground, he elbowed me in the throat, and done his best to gouge out my eyes.

As his bony fingers scratched at my eyes, a wave of panic swept over me. Raising up my knee, I levered him over, getting on top. Trying to hold him down with my knee, I pounded my fist into his face. I swatted him a couple of pretty good licks before he threw me off.

His eyes wild and his breathing ragged, Eastham tried to smash my knee with his boot. Dodging back, I set my feet and pasted him square in the nose.

Holding his nose, the big doctor staggered back, smacking into the wall of the saloon. For a long time, he stood there, his chest heaving as he held his smashed nose. Slowly he brought his hand down, his eyes widening at the sight of his own blood.

His eyes flashing wildly, he flipped his wrist, the tiny derringer shooting into his hand. Now, that little pistol might not look like much, not until it's headed your way in the hand of a man with pure hate in his eyes. Right then and there that little gun looked as big as a howitzer.

Holding my hands in front of me, I backed away, knowing Eastham wasn't bluffing this time. He'd seen his plans go down the drain, and I reckon he blamed me. This time, he wasn't trying to bluff me into signing some paper. This time he meant to kill me. He was just milking the moment.

I backed away another step, looking around wildly for something, anything, I could use to defend myself. I spied Eastham's Colt lying a few feet from my feet. Only a few short feet away, but it might as well been on the moon for all the good it was going to do me.

Before I could dive for it, get the gun, and fire, Eastham would have time for a cup of coffee and a smoke before he killed me. There wasn't a chance, but still, I was going to make a try. I done decided that. I'd rather die making a try at that gun than beg him.

I looked from the gun back to Eastham. He smiled his teeth bloody. ''Go ahead, Sheriff. There it is. Go for it. Who knows? You might even make it,'' he taunted.

I tensed my muscles, taking a slow deep breath trying to work up my nerve. Keyed up tight as a fiddle string, I watched Eastham's face. His eyes narrowed as his finger tightened on the trigger.

Before Eastham could fire, a half-dozen horseshoes rained off the top of the saloon, driving the big doctor to his knees. Before he had a chance to recover, I dove for the gun. Snatching up that pistol, I rolled over and fired in one easy motion, and I kept firing till the gun was empty.

Those bullets smashed Eastham back against the wall of the saloon, pinning him there. As my gun ran empty, Eastham slid down the wall, the derringer dribbling from his fingers.

The whole town became quiet as death as I slowly climbed to my feet, ramming the pistol down in my pants. I glanced up to the roof of the saloon to see Eddy standing there, holding her last horseshoe. Waving, she smiled down at me and gave me a small salute.

Feeling older than Moses' goat, I returned the wave and let the pistol slip through my fingers.

Chapter Eighteen

We spent the rest of the day rounding up East-ham's men and tying them up in the jail. Turley didn't help, he went right back to his doctoring. He patched up Wiesmulluer's dog. Shoot, he liked the way the castor oil worked so good, he even gave the dog a snort of it.

By morning, most of the sick folks were feeling better. Now, I don't know if it was Turley's cure, or the knowledge that the railroad was coming to town, but something put color back into their cheeks.

The railroad. That was the main topic of conversation in Whiskey City. Folks began to speculate on how much our land was going to be worth.

All except for Wiesmulluer, he didn't do nothing but coo over his sick dog. He fetched the old mutt food and water all day. I swear, I think he liked that dog better than any human.

Andrews tried to buy all the land he could, but nobody was selling. I reckon we all figured on being rich. I had to smile at ol' Andrews. For a man who was sick over the trouble his greed caused, he sure got the hankering to make money again mighty quick. I guess it's true, a leopard don't change its spots.

Andrews avoided me at first. Then finally he cut me out of the ground. "Teddy, I've been meaning to speak with you." He ducked his head and went to fussin' and frettin'. "Well, I just wanted to thank you for what you did." He looked off to the south and scrunched up his face. "And I want to thank you for not telling folks how I helped Eastham move in here."

"Think nothing of it," I said, then coulda kicked myself. I shoulda let the pudgy little sucker squirm for a few more days, just to learn him a lesson. I sighed. I might as well put him at ease. "I know you didn't mean for anybody to get hurt. You was just trying to make a dollar."

A big grin split his face as he pounded me on the back. "That's right. Now, I've got this deal. . . . "

Three days after Eastham's raid, we loaded our prisoners for the trip to Central City, where they could be turned over to the Federal Marshals.

Me and Turley figured on escorting the prisoners by ourselves, but that wasn't the way it turned out. The whole town turned out, gussied up in their Sunday best, all set for the trip to town.

"Are you sure you folks are up to this trip?" I asked, looking across their shining faces.

"We feel fine," Iris said. "Josh told us the railroad had an office in Central City and we mean to see the man in charge."

I tried to talk them out of it, but them folks were dead set on going. I finally gave in, figuring if Eastham couldn't kill these folks, a little ride wasn't going to polish them off.

It was a tight fit, but we squeezed into three wagons. Iris started to get into the lead wagon with Eddy and me, but then she stopped, glancing all about. "Where's Gid?" she muttered, then let out a wicked scream. "Gid, quit flapping your gums and get out here. We're ready to leave."

Believe me, Gid appeared mighty quick. He came lumbering out of the saloon toting a big basket. "Sorry, dear, I was just getting some glasses for the lemonade you made."

Iris smiled and brushed some lint from Gid's suitcoat. "That's very thoughtful, dear," she said, then she kissed him! Wow! Imagine that. Old Iris actually kissing somebody. They held hands as Gid helped her into the back of the wagon.

I reckon my mouth was hanging open a foot as I urged the horses into motion. I never seen Iris so sweet in all my days. Even Eddy looked a mite shocked.

"Teddy, I don't think we have properly thanked you for all you done," Iris said as we rolled out of town.

I looked at the old girl out of the corner of my eyes. I swear, she was being so nice, it was almost scary. "Don't think nothing of it, ma'am. I was just doing my job."

"Well, you did it well," Iris said primly.

"You sure did," Gid agreed. He leaned forward and slapped me on the back. "I'm right proud of you, boy."

"I'm proud of you too," Eddy whispered, leaning her head on my shoulder.

"If anyone gets hungry, I've packed a lunch," Iris offered and pointed to the basket beside Gid. Then she and Gid went to whispering and giggling like a couple of schoolkids.

By the time we reached Central City, I was ready for the old Iris to come back. This new Iris was so sweet it was sickening. Besides, I didn't trust her. I figured she'd snap under the strain before long.

We left our prisoners at the jail. Then the whole bunch of us trooped down the street, looking for the railroad office. Once we found it, we stormed the place.

The man behind the desk looked up quickly, dropping his spectacles as he saw the bunch of us crowding into his office. "You the railroad man?" Andrews demanded.

"Yes, Sidney Lowe, at your service. How may I help you fine people?"

"We are from Whiskey City, and we want to know how much you are going to pay us to put a station in our town," Blanche Caster demanded.

Lowe placed his glasses back on his nose, adjusting them several times. "I regret that you have been misinformed. We are not planning to pay for the land we use." The little man wilted a bit under our hot glare. He wiped his brow and adjusted his glasses again. "The railroad is short of funds. We are asking the people to donate the land for the tracks. We feel that by working together we can build this railroad, which will greatly benefit all involved."

"You thought wrong!" Iris snapped, looking like her old self. She leaned across the desk, and, for just a second, I thought she would pull Lowe over the desk and tan his backside. "We came here to sell land, not give it away."

Lowe spread his hands in front of him. "I am truly sorry, but I have explained our position." He leaned across the desk, his eyes meeting Iris's. "Surely you can see the benefits of having the railroad coming through your town?''

Lowe had a point and we all knew it, we just didn't like letting go of the idea that we was going to be rich. Finally, we gave in, signing a paper allowing the tracks to be built across our land.

''Outstanding,'' Lowe said as the last man signed the paper. ''Now, allow me to buy you a drink. Let's retire to the saloon and you can name your poison. I'm buying.''

Poison!

Like a herd of hogs, we bolted out of that place and didn't stop until we were home.